MOUSE TRAPPED

MOUSE TRAPPED

Sandy Dengler

VICTOR BOOKS
A DIVISION OF SCRIPTURE PRESS PUBLICATIONS INC.
USA CANADA ENGLAND

Copyediting: Carole Streeter and Barbara Williams
Cover Design: Paul Higdon
Cover Illustration: John Dawson

Library of Congress Cataloging-in-Publication Data

Dengler, Sandy.
Mouse trapped / by Sandy Dengler.
p. cm. —(Mirage mysteries; 2)
ISBN 1-56476-136-3
I. Title. II. Series: Dengler, Sandy. Mirage mysteries; 2.
PS3554.E524M68 1993
813' .54—dc20 93-10406
CIP

1 2 3 4 5 6 7 8 9 10 Printing/Year 97 96 95 94 93

Contents

Mouse

He felt like grime on a bridal gown, like a slug on a strawberry.

Joe Rodriguez strode the length of the basement hall in the E wing of Mays Memorial. It didn't help that six minutes ago he'd been waxing his car. His wet jogging shoes squished as he walked. He looked and smelled like a mess. Faces he did not know eyed him suspiciously as he passed, despite the fact that he had hung his badge conspicuously from his belt.

Cleanliness, they say, is a state of mind. Hospitals are supposed to be crisp and clean, but Mays Memorial raised cleanliness from mere state of mind to the linchpin of existence. From the candy stripers in seersucker to the staff in white or scrub green, every man jack looked as if he/she had just stepped out of the pages of a uniform catalog. The walls glistened bright, the floors shone glass smooth. Stainless steel prevailed; no wood dared show its warmth.

He knocked at 18E and entered unbidden. He was no longer the only unclean person in the universe. Three nurses and two doctors were working on a quiet form in bloodied clothing. As Joe swung wide around the foot of the table, he noted that only the lower half of the form was clothed. Her T-shirt and bra had been cut away and a nurse was hacking at the bloody jeans.

Dr. Lee Asimoto raised a beckoning finger toward Joe and pointed to the head of the table. "He's here already, Marsha. Told you he wouldn't dilly-dally."

Joe stepped in beside the nurse fiddling with Marsha's IV bag. "When Lee says to hustle, the world speeds up. Hello, Mouse."

She forced a wan smile, so he reached to take her hand in his. He lifted her oxygen mask enough to let her speak. "Hi, Joe. You shouldn't see me like this. Ain't decent."

"You look much better than I expected."

"Really?" Her voice rasped low, barely perceptible. "I feel terrible . . . like I'm gonna die. Joe, get next door and talk to that guy, if you can. He didn't get a chance to say anything to me. Maybe you can get something."

"What do you have, since I'm here?"

"Nothing."

"What happened?"

"A phone tip . . . I can't think straight. They gave me something . . . A tipster called Pete about a major lift. Silver and turquoise. Wanted to sell the tip. Pete gave me fifty bucks. I went to the contact point. He was supposed to tell me when and where. On the heist. The tipster got there same time I did. I showed him the fifty and my karate belt. Just in case he thought he'd take the money. . . ." She inhaled deeply. "Money and run, y'know? Then bang, bang. He's down and I'm down."

"Who went first?"

"So fast. I think him."

"How many shots?"

"Don' know. Four. At least four. Four or five."

"From where?"

"Don' know."

"The tipster mention any names?"

"No time. No."

"Any sudden fear on his face? Shock of recognition? Any sign he saw the assailant? That a known person was nearby?"

"No. Surprise."

"Any vehicles? Suspicious loiterers? Anything odd?"

She tried to move her head and couldn't. She was turning whiter.

Joe gave her hand a squeeze. "Don't let Lee sell you any of those raffle tickets for the free sukiyaki dinners. It's that time of year again." He nestled her rebreather close around her face and backed away. Instantly a nurse stepped in between him and Mouse's tousled head.

Dr. Asimoto caught his eye and scowled. "Sixteen next door. Hustle."

Joe walked outside. He paused a moment in the bright hallway to clear his lungs of the smell of blood and sweat and vomit and then entered 16E.

The doctor attending the second victim was new to the staff of Mays; Joe had met him only once. He was almost a handspan shorter than Joe's five-eleven, his ego a pound or two cockier. He probably matched Joe's 175 ounce to ounce.

"Dr. Hausmann? Joe Rodriguez, homicide."

"We met before. I remember you. A bit premature, aren't you? He's still alive."

"We occasionally stoop to investigating attempted murders if our in-basket's empty." Joe warned himself in vain to keep this young man from rankling. "Can he speak?"

"Doubt it."

Joe moved in close to the victim's head. He glanced at the nurse across the table, a cute little redhead. The eyes were familiar, but she was fixing her hair differently now. It took him a moment to connect. "Jennifer Fugate, isn't it? You used to work at Scottsdale Memorial."

Her face lit up like Christmas. "Very good, Mr. Rodriguez! It is, and I did. That was almost a year ago. Nice to see you again."

"And you." Joe bent down close to the man's face. The boy was young—surely less than twenty-one—and until five minutes ago had sported a scraggly blond beard. Now he sported only half a beard, for bullets had torn his right cheek, side, and abdomen. He looked even more drained and moribund than Mouse.

"Can you hear me?" Joe pinched the man's ear. Nothing.

Across from him, Jennifer licked her lips. She glanced sideways at Dr. Hausmann who was busy with the abdominal wound. She lifted her eyebrows at Joe and took the boy's hand. Her fingers moved. If that was a hypodermic needle in her hand—if she was literally sticking pins under the boy's fingernails—Joe didn't want to know about it. It was working, whatever it was; the boy's head rolled.

"Who did this? Who shot you?"

The blue lips worked. He was awake enough to be trying. He had heard. "Bren . . . Burr . . . en . . . sss . . . Brrr . . ." A deep breath; "Berrennnzzz . . . ssss . . ." The breathing ceased.

Dr. Hausmann snapped his fingers. "Don't just stand around watching the evening news, plug him in! He's dead. Come on; come on! Step on it!"

Joe stood back as green scrubs swarmed around the table. The doors whipped open and a sanitized orderly wheeled in a white machine.

Long minutes later, Dr. Hausmann stepped back.

Joe moved in beside him. "Not hopeful, I take it."

"Too many things torn apart inside. We could rebuild the jaw and palate, fix him up some false teeth. But we're fresh out of livers and kidneys and spleens. You got all you'll ever get out of him. Surprised you got that much. He must really hate that Brent Whoever."

"I'll be next door with Asimoto in 18." Joe turned, stopped and turned back again. "Liver, kidneys, spleen. How many shots?"

"Two."

"Musta been an odd angle to do all that damage."

"Right. When you have time to leave your in-basket and look for snipers, start with upstairs windows."

"Appreciate it. Thank you, doctor." Joe left.

He paused in the hallway to press fingers on his own body where the boy's wounds occurred. In order to take out the aforementioned organs, he calculated the bullets would have to travel at an angle of. . . . A blur of white hovered nearby. A sweet little trick, no doubt fresh out of nursing school, was standing there staring at him. He nodded to her and slipped hastily through the doors of 18.

Joe sat in Pete Marks' chair and stretched his feet out under Pete's desk because this was the only vacant chair in robbery, and Pete wasn't here anyway. Burly Purley Petersen sat jabbing at a computer keyboard two desks down, his fingertips bigger than the keys. Robbery was one of the busiest of details and seemed crammed into the dingiest, smallest of squad rooms. Joe's own quarters weren't much more appealing, but he mentally thanked the Lord for what he had.

Pete's chair was built for him, not Joe. Pete was much bigger, broad as well as long, with an age-belly. His heavy bottom had over the years shaped the chair padding to his conformity. In fact, nothing about Pete was like Joe. Compare Pete's gray burr to Joe's longer black hair, or Pete's red I-hate-the-sun face with Joe's dark born-for-the-sun coloring.

An unruly shock of red hair over an olive-green shirt popped in the far door. Joe raised an arm as his lanky, nonstop partner came bobbing across the room, greeting each female present by name.

"Jose, me lad, what be ye doing in this dump?"

Tom Flaherty flashed a toothy grin at Purley and parked on the corner of Pete's desk.

"Slumming." Joe leaned forward a bit for a closer look. "Missed a spot shaving this morning."

"More than one morning. Haven't ye noticed? Be starting meself a moustache."

"That's a relief. I thought you were overfertilizing your nose hair." Joe leaned back again. "Seen Pete yet?"

"No, and his car's not in its slot. Alloo, Purley."

"Tommy. Heard anything new?"

"No. The tipster's name is Lawrence Banks. Got that off his prints. He called from a pay phone at a minimart on Sixteenth and Osborn."

"Two blocks from the shooting." Joe was starting to feel an inexplicable heaviness, a foreboding.

Purley gave up typing and came over to perch on the other corner of Pete's desk. The desk made little creaking noises beneath his 280 pounds of bulk.

"Aye," Tom stretched his lanky legs out before him. It was definitely his legs that gave him his six-foot-one of height; were they in proportion to his body, he'd be shorter than Joe. "I just listened to the tape of the phone conversation. The lad promised Pete inside info on a major liberation of Indian jewelry. Not your piddling Tiffany's robbery, but a biggie."

Purley scowled. "What could be bigger than a jewelry store?"

"Something that sells Indian stuff. One of the shops downtown, or out in Scottsdale. There be dozens there."

Joe studied the tops of his boots. His Wellingtons

felt a lot more comfortable than did those wet canvas shoes an hour ago. He probably should have changed before he left for the hospital. No, then he would not have gotten the garbled "brendzz" out of the boy, for Lawrence Banks was dead now.

"Silver and turquoise." Joe stared at Purley, thinking out loud. "Not necessarily *selling* the stuff. How about *collecting* Indian art and jewelry?"

Tom brightened. "The very thing! Like mayhap Mrs. Thompson's Royce Howard collection. An impressive array, that."

"Heldt Museum," Purley added. "What's its full name? Heldt Collection of Indian Art and Antiquities?"

Tom pulled Pete's phone off the hook and punched a couple of extension numbers.

"I understand," said Joe, "that the Phoenix Art Museum has a temporary display of classic Indian silver this month. One of those traveling exhibits."

Purley nodded. "You have to hold tickets to get into that one. Their security's tighter 'n a dowager's girdle. Too hard to reach."

Joe considered that aspect. "They're all hard to reach. Heldt's security system is an oldie but goodie. And some of these private collections are better protected than the museums. Maybe a collection out of town. Any hints the heist has to happen here in Phoenix?" He glanced across at Tom who had heard firsthand the tape of the tipster's conversation, but the Irishman was concentrating on the telephone. He grunted, nodding to the person on the other end of the line.

Purley shrugged. "Incidentally, Joe, I hope we're

together on this one."

"I imagine so. The lieutenant's on vacation—went up to Colorado for two weeks—but I don't see why not. The boy's dead; that's us. Mel Carter is heading it up officially, but Tommy and I and everyone else are chipping in. And we're dealing with robbery. That's you. We'll be a lot more efficient pooling our efforts, I'd think."

"Good. Now I have a suggestion. Let's make the rounds of the major collections. I know the assistant director at the art museum. His name's Brent Sommers, and he's in charge of . . ." Purley's eyes grew wide. "That garble the kid made!" He wagged his head. "Wouldn't it be something? Come up with the culprit first lick off the lollipop? Can't be this Sommers, though. He's too smooth to shoot people. He's in charge of the temporary and traveling exhibits, both going and coming. And I know the owner of Crenshaw's Indian Store downtown here."

"Tommy knows that Mrs. Thompson personally. And Heldt's on my way to the Carver Cadillac Agency. Carver has a dandy collection in their back room. The problem with lifting a collection, Burl, is fencing. You should know the good outlets."

"We have a few names in our notebook. No one really skilled at getting the most out of a museum collection that I know of, but we'll work that angle hard."

Tom cradled the phone and stretched agonizingly. "Banks' police record is forthcoming for our perusal."

Joe felt like yawning and suppressed it. "We're

going to let the prime targets in town know we're expecting a major rip-off, Tommy. Might keep 'em on their toes just a little sharper. What's new with Hennie?"

Tom snapped to standing and wandered over to a printer beyond Purley's desk as it sprang to life ticking lickety-split. "Her eldest son just passed his bar exams. Her baby boy, the fourteen-year-old with one diamond stud earring, won his school's computer derby. Here we go."

He watched the machine perform its magic a few more moments, then ripped off a printout three pages long. He plopped it down on Pete's desk where everyone could see it.

Purley ran his pudgy finger down the page. "Breaking and entering, second-story work, burglary—except one possession of grass—suspended. And four parking violations in the last month."

"Where?" Joe craned his neck and still he couldn't see well.

Tom's long, skinny finger took over. "Strange places, strange times of day. Buckeye Road at 3 A.M.; Baseline in Tempe, midnight; Van Buren downtown last week; Saints in Skagway! Look there!"

"Wish I could," said Joe, but no one heard.

"Eleven last night our luckless parker picked up another one on Twenty-fourth near Thomas." Tommy looked at Joe. "Just cleared the computers, looks like; one of those ye-mustn't-park-one-night-of-the-week-because-the-street-cleaner's-coming—and he did."

Purley grunted. "Bet the city don't collect the fine

on that one."

"Harley and Turk working his friends and family?" Joe twisted the printout around to reading angle.

"Aye, what there be of them. Harry Wallace too. Notified an uncle in Show Low; that's the only family we can find."

The feeling of foreboding behind Joe's breastbone intensified. The door at the far end opened. Pete was back and the room turned chill. Joe knew what he was going to say; probably everyone in the room could tell. The message zapped like electricity, unspoken.

Pete quietly addressed the room in general. No need to raise his voice; everyone was listening. Everyone knew. "Mouse died fifteen minutes ago."

Pete

Ah, June. Tender green grass. The first blush of summer bloom. Robins warbling happily as tiny wrens set up housekeeping in exotic nest sites. Bullhooie. Every bit of it bullhooie when you're observing June in Phoenix.

The soft green grass of spring has come and gone already, leaving only the ovenproof Bermuda grass to bear the brunt of summer. The spring flowers have withered down to naked brown stalks as an overbearing sun turns the sidewalks into griddles. The robins all go north to more agreeable summer climes and won't be back till fall. And the wrens of Phoenix – raucous, extroverted cactus wrens – are the size of starlings. They can't even sing like wrens; the best they can do is a harsh squawk. And they nest in cactus.

Joe stood on the sidewalk and felt the heat warm

the leather soles of his boots. June in Phoenix... nothing to write poems about.

The main TV people were gone, probably back at the studio editing like mad for the evening news. Skeleton TV crews with minicams wandered about like jackals, in case some scrap of news should chance to fall. The whole street was roped off, but civilian rubberneckers were standing around under the palm trees on the lawn of the Valley National Bank across the street. Why do banks go in for such grotesque architecture? Valley's roof swooped in five or six directions; its billious curves made you queasy just looking at it.

Joe watched awhile as Maynard Rust's lab people wrapped up their thing, but his mind kept wandering elsewhere. Two people, one of them a young officer with rich promise, had died here on this toasty sidewalk.

Marsha Mouse. He didn't even know her last name. She was always simply Mouse over in Robbery. Five feet even, 88 pounds, maybe, if she was wearing extra clothing, stick-out ears she hid in her hair, absolutely huge brown eyes.

Pete's protegé, Mouse was. It was he who had brought her from jail duty over to the detective division, served as her mentor, sent her off to various law enforcement training courses. Theirs was not an illicit relationship, everyone agreed. Pete was happily married. It was a father-daughter thing with Pete ever the proud parent.

The boy, Lawrence Banks, raised interesting question marks. He probably would not have been able to respond without Jennifer Fugate's assistance, but respond he did. To what value? He was a good-looking kid, tanned, well built. And according to Harry, he had been essentially friendless.

And Pete Marks. Robbery was a feudal estate where Pete reigned as lord over all. Mouse's loss tore Pete up terribly; Joe could understand that. What he did not understand was the way Pete turned from ashen gray to livid red two hours ago, when he saw Joe sitting in his chair—the way he ranted for three minutes over Joe's unforgivable transgression of sitting at his desk. No doubt he had to vent his frustration somewhere and Joe, by random reason, was "it." Joe didn't do too well at psychological analysis. That was more Tom's department.

Mel Carter, his handsome face awash in sweat, his sandy hair tousled and his shirt perspiration-stained, came out the door of the abandoned storefront and stopped beside Joe. "How can you look so cool in that coat?"

"You've been away from Pennsylvania for years. Haven't you acclimated yet? You're coordinating this one, right?"

Mel breathed a heartfelt vulgarity. "It's not just the sun heat, Joe. It's *all* the heat. This case is going down the tubes and it's the one case the department doesn't dare screw up. And I get stuck with it."

"What's going wrong?"

"Everything. Mouse had backup, you know that? Two uniformed officers half a block away. And by the time they got here, the perp was gone."

"Sounds like they didn't cover in close enough."

"And I nearly drew my weapon on Pete Marks,

trying to make him keep himself where he belongs. He's been in and out of the scene, tracking dirt everywhere, roaring around. He destroyed the scene and he's messing everybody else up. And you know what, Joe? If I shot him dead, I don't think he'd notice. He'd keep right on slamming around." Mel's arms exploded outward in a fling of frustration. "Why me?"

A blond head appeared in the open window above the vacant store. She called Joe's name and motioned to him to come up.

Mel glanced up at her. "Go ahead, Joe. The place is as picked over and as wrecked as it's going to be. You can't do anything more to it." He wandered off muttering.

Joe flapped an acknowledgment up to Gretchen and crossed the sidewalk, sidestepping Doug Hakamura and his measuring tape. Carefully he avoided the two black, caking blotches and entered a broken door. He eventually had to climb the fire escape steps to find a way to the right room.

Tall, blond Gretchen Wiemer stood in the middle of the room reloading her camera. "We've got the place pretty well done, but we're going to seal it anyway. Your sniper was here, Joe."

"I deny possession. Mel's complaining about Pete. What's going on?"

Gretchen's face softened. "Like his own daughter, Joe. And I don't know how to help him, which shoulder to pat, what to say. Nothing."

"Me neither, except to let him unload on me when he feels like erupting. How do you know this is the place?"

She walked over to the window. "Nothing as corny as shell casings left behind or anything, but see how the dust on the windowsill is disturbed here? And the floor?"

"Got all your samples?"

"Yeah."

"Prints?"

"Footprints, inconclusive. I wanted them to wait for you—you perform miracles with tracking; but the dust on the floor was too muddied up."

"Pete."

"And a half dozen other cops who ought to know better. You might go over what we have, if you would. We dusted for fingers and found zip. Here, look at this. Notice how he'd have to lean way out there in order to get a clear shot at either of them." She stepped aside.

"Who has access to the building?"

"The world. There's the front door and two doors facing the alley, both missing."

"So the killer didn't have to plan in advance to come here."

"Premeditated or spur-of-the-moment. You pays your money and you takes your pick."

Joe grunted. He stood at the window, hefted an imaginary pistol, and aimed at the sidewalk. It didn't feel right. "Doug? Hey, Doug?"

Broad, stocky Hakamura stopped and looked up.

"How was Banks positioned when he was hit?"

Doug walked down the sidewalk twenty feet, turned, eyeballed his route, stepped out and started walking. He stopped beside a blotch. "Bang."

"And Mouse?"

He realigned himself and walked down the street, out near the curb. He stopped near the black spot and looked up at Joe. "Bang."

"Thanks, Doug." Joe pulled his head back inside to study the window framing. "Gretch. Right here."

"Right where?" She stared at the frame. "Smudged, sorta. A few splinters loosened. Hard to see unless you're looking for it." She grinned. "I got it! He held onto the frame here, hung out the window and fired. That means he's probably left-handed, since he had to hang on with his right."

"At the very least forced into left-handedness by the positions of his victims. It's a bad angle." Joe sighed. "If Mouse had stayed in close to the buildings, he couldn't have hit her at all."

"Hindsight. Ladies' safety rule number one – stay clear of buildings or shrubbery or anything where a guy might pop out and grab you. She was doing it right, theoretically." Her voice faltered. "Joe, why am I so scared?"

"I don' know. Maybe because Mouse got it in daylight on a safe street with no warning, on a routine, nondangerous assignment with backup."

"Yeah. Guess so." She was pale. He had never seen Gretchen Wiemer, militant feminist, frightened before, let alone fearstruck. He held out his hand and she laid hers in it. The temperature was on top of 100 and her hand felt damp and clammy. He drew her in and wrapped his arms tightly around her. She stood nearly as tall as he, and even with low heels met him eye to eye. No matter. Just now she was a frightened little girl in need of shelter from a threatening world.

She melted in against him. "We were friends, y'know that?"

"You and Mouse."

Her head, scrunched down on his shoulder, nodded. "We'd go over to the bruise room together, or out on the range. Commit mayhem on each other. Practice karate. She was brown belt. Almost ten inches shorter than me and she threw me constantly. Fun times, Joe."

"I'm beginning to appreciate a little better how Pete feels."

"She didn't know it was coming. It wasn't supposed to be coming. She was wearing her grubbies just so she wouldn't look like a cop when she made the contact. There wasn't any reason . . ." She stopped, but not, apparently, to cry. She clung, snuffled, and clung tighter. Joe wished for her sake that she'd just dissolve and get it over with.

And his own feelings weighed just as heavy. Besides the few moments of his initial conversation with Mouse, he spent another couple minutes with her later, until they trundled her off to surgery. Not once did he mention anything about Jesus Christ or salvation, despite the fact that she was close to death. Not once. It didn't even occur to him to say something until it seemed like too late. And now . . .

He kept her snuggled in close. "If you don't want to be alone, why don't you spend a couple days over at my sister's? Be around people. Besides, the kids have been badgering us to get them a dog, and we need help choosing."

"No. Thanks. I'll be fine. I appreciate it, though, I really do."

Doug Hakamura appeared in the doorway and crossed the room, leading his assistant on the other end of his measuring tape.

Joe was about to say something when Pete Marks himself filled the doorway. Pete scowled in silence, black as a mountain thunderstorm. He wheeled and disappeared.

Gretchen shuddered a wrenching sigh and motioned with a nod of her head toward one of the assistants. They walked over to the window.

Doug blinked at the empty doorway. "Now what was all that?"

"I don't know." The sense of foreboding had in no way diminished. It lingered as strong as ever in the depths of Joe's chest. "But until Pete gets over this a little, I imagine we're going to see a lot of what-was-all-that."

SHADOWS

Once upon a time, when Joe was very small and the moon was new, his father took him along in their rickety pickup truck down to Guadelupe. In the darkness of that sultry night, his father and he joined a half dozen Yaqui men and as many boys around a campfire up a shallow and silent draw. Half a mile down the wash, in town, kids yelled and dogs barked and cattle lowed. Out here an eerie separateness haunted them. Vivid black shadows counterpointed the dancing yellow flames; there were no shades of gray, no middle ground. This night belonged to the darkness.

The men told each other ghost stories, tales of the supernatural involving Aztec gold and Yaqui silver. Hair-raising tales they were, of demons and slavering monsters who protected the spendid silverwork of murdered Yaqui artists. Joe's father, being half Yaqui and half Mexican, could tell stories of either culture. Since both cultures suffered near annihilation by the hands of the Europeans, and since a hatred of white greed seethed unquenched, the stories melded into each other in Joe's memory. Gold. Silver. Silver. Gold. The most finely wrought pieces carried the heaviest load of curse and evil.

One of the storytellers at that campfire died a few months later of lung cancer. A couple of others moved down to Mexico. They never assembled again, but the stories themselves were branded onto Joe's heart. Now he couldn't think about silverwork without thinking about the weight of unseen lore that accompanied it.

Mouse was going to pick up a tip about a major haul of silver. He wondered if any Yaqui pieces might be among that haul, and whether the ancient curses and monsters could be busily at work here already, killing with their legendary reckless abandon. His mother had emigrated from Chelsea near London. His English side huffily disputed the theory, agreeing with his left brain that that was stuff and nonsense. And all the while, his North American heritage continued to whisper dark suggestions.

He stood on the sidewalk beside two blotches of fried blood. He didn't want to go back to the office and the heavy pall that hung there. He had nothing left to do here. Mel Carter was signing the scene off, element by element. Joe was a bystander.

Very few people still wandered about beyond the tape. The last of the TV crews had disappeared. End of event. Joe studied the curb a few moments, dragging back into memory what he'd noticed when first he arrived . . . there by the Valley National Bank, a tall, brown-haired, gangly kid in a black T-shirt, twenty to twenty-five years old. He was still standing there now. What was the fascination about this crime scene that would hold the attention of a young man for nearly an hour?

Joe flagged Mel down and told him in undertones what he was up to. Mel pulled his radio as he turned away.

Joe came down off the curb and stepped over the tape. Without actually looking at the kid in the black T-shirt, he walked toward the general direction of the bank with its bilious roof. The kid watched him intently for a few moments. Then, like a spooked fawn, he wheeled and began walking briskly toward the bank parking lot. Joe altered direction and picked up the pace.

The kid glanced guiltily over his shoulder at Joe and upped his gait to a jog. Now why would a perfectly innocent bystander get so worried just because some plainclothes officer crossed the street toward him?

When the kid broke into a run, so did Joe. And it surprised him how cathartic running can be, especially when you're after someone who is fast becoming an interesting suspect.

A metro unit, its Mars bar flashing red and blue, came screeching around the corner. It pulled to the curb and two uniformed officers hopped out. The kid turned away from them, which put him at an angle to Joe. He headed straight for a six-foot cinder-block wall. With a mighty, scrambling lunge, the kid squirmed and wriggled up and over. He crashed into a hedge of oleanders planted against the other side.

Six-foot brick walls are standard furniture on your average police training obstacle course. Ever since a perp ran over him, literally, two years ago, Joe had trouble with walls. His right hand did not grip, and it's always nice to be able to grip the top. His right leg lacked strength; any jumping Joe did had to be with his left leg.

Janet James, the only female detective currently in homicide, had shown Joe how to do it. "Like you're getting on a horse bareback," she explained, which meant nothing. Joe could count on one hand the number of times he'd ridden a horse and still have enough fingers left to peel a banana. So she demonstrated, keeping her shoulders low and flinging her hips and one leg up over. Joe had seen that done in *Dances with Wolves*.

He hit the wall now as Janet had demonstrated, gripping with his good hand and keeping his shoulders level, swinging his good leg up and over. The cops behind him had jumped back into their unit. The flashing lights whipped by. As he arched himself onto the top and rolled off into the oleanders, he glimpsed the black T-shirt, like a dark shadow, less than fifty yards away.

He fought his way out of the shrubbery and found himself in the back lot of one of the biggest nurseries in town. Potted saplings stood in row upon orderly row, and bagged palm trees were stacked along the back fence. The trees, plus the scores of free-standing racks of bedding plants, winter vegetables, and ground covers, gave the kid a zillion places to hide, and Joe had no idea if there was a weapon involved here.

Their sirens howling, units converged on the two driveway entrances. Mel was throwing the whole city of Phoenix into this, a strong indication of how desperate he was.

Joe was sweating now. The exertion made him feel good . . . or at least better. He was doing something, physically doing something about those two black splotches on the sidewalk. It bode well that this horrific case was getting off with a bang.

All the customers apparently were shopping for their plants inside the air-conditioned store. The lot stood vacant, devoid of sound or motion. Joe paused stock-still in the middle of the lot, and listened. Nothing but silence. No movements except for the backup swarming all around the edges. Cops now rimmed the lot completely; at least a half dozen of them moved along its outer periphery, weapons in hand.

Joe walked over to where he had last seen the black T-shirt and dropped down. The dirt here was packed hard from millions of feet and millions of night waterings. But there were the traces of the kid's passage, not so much footprints as vague footmarks—a slight gouge here, a scuff there. He stooped low, shading his eyes from the glare, and started tracking.

Joe winced whenever someone claimed he was the best tracker the department had ever had. He much preferred to be considered one of the best thinkers. The department held thinking in low regard, however, when it came to scoping the scene around some corpse in the desert, or finding a lost child down in South Mountain Park. And now, with a scared kid hiding somewhere among a jungle of plants, the arcane skills of his father and his father before him came in pretty handy.

He stood erect. The kid had changed directions here, ducking aside down an aisle between two tall free-standing racks of geraniums. He probably cowered somewhere within thirty feet of Joe this very minute.

Joe drew his weapon, aimed it two-handed approximately at heaven, and addressed the silence around him. "You in the black T-shirt beyond the geraniums there. You're digging yourself into a deeper hole than you can get out of. Cut your losses now by coming out into the open with your hands on your head."

The plant rack right in front of him exploded and came slamming at him, slinging geranium pots. As it tipped against him, it knocked over the rack behind him, a domino effect with him on the botton. He covered his face with his arms and tried to roll out into the main aisle, free of the chaos. A couple of those flying geranium pots hit him and he could suddenly understand how St. Stephen could die by stoning. All but his slow leg made it clear of the noisy crash.

Cops yelled and came running. Joe yanked his leg free, leaving his Wellington behind under the debris. The black T-shirt was headed for the side fence beyond the stacked palm trees. Joe rolled to his feet and took off after him.

He carried his gun in his good left hand; dropping it now would prove embarrassing, if not fatal. He hollered to the kid to freeze, but both of them knew he had no teeth in his bite. What he needed was a clear line of fire, not so he could shoot at the kid but so he could order him down. The black T-shirt ducked behind the palm trunks.

Joe yelled, "The alley!" as the kid went up and over the cyclone fence at the back of the lot. Cops shouted to cops off at the far end.

When the city garbage folk switched from conventional trash cans to those four-foot green plastic cans on wheels, they collected not in the alleys anymore but out on the street, where their trucks could pull up beside and dump the cans with remote-control claws. The city abandoned the alleys as useless. It was just one such useless alley into which the kid escaped. By the time the cops could plug the ends and root him out of the head-high salt cedar and oleander, he had probably crossed three other fences.

Joe went over the cyclone fence as he had gone over the wall, but not nearly in time. When Joe plus five winded cops converged upon one another, with no black-shirted shadow between them, the hunt was over. He started tracking again, painstakingly working his way from mark to mark in the rock-hard dirt; but following a vague trail is infinitely slower than the person making that trail.

On impulse he began backtracking, following every move the kid made, looking for any physical evidence. He found a pencil stub, maybe four inches long, close to the cyclone fence. Before he bagged it, he got down on his knees with one ear on the ground to make sure from the dirt around it that the pencil had been dropped this afternoon. He continued on past the fallen racks and nearly lost the trail because it was so obscured by the tracks of the gawkers. Every clerk and customer was out here now, milling around and messing up the scene.

And then he found the keys. When the kid went over that first brick wall, he lost a ring of keys. Joe was smugly admiring his find when Mel wandered over.

Mel was not smug. "You lost him. What? You some small-town yokel?" He caught himself and sighed. "Sorry. I keep forgetting you're a sergeant. My apologies."

"No problem. I'm frustrated too."

"Only guilt could make that kid hang around the scene and then run when approached. I want him, Joe."

"So do I." Joe dangled the keys on the end of his pen before he dropped them in the bag.

"How do you know they're his?" Mel wrinkled his nose.

"From the patterning of the dust where they fell, they were dropped within the last two hours. Nothing has settled around them or on them yet. None of our people went over this particular wall besides me, and they're not mine."

Mel grunted. "Okay. So who is he?"

"Let's find out."

From time to time, outside agencies who use the department's lab facility complain about how slowly results come back. They fail to realize it is all a matter of priorities.

The key ring was a priority. Gretchen got nothing useful off the pencil, but within moments of opening the key bag, she lifted a nice thumbprint and some partials from the first finger—about what you'd expect from keys. And she opened the bag within moments of receiving it.

Then all other work ceased. Everyone—Doug Hakamura, Gretchen, Mel, Tommy, and Joe—stood around with their hands in their pockets, figuratively or literally, staring at that innocuous ring of keys lying on the lab table.

Joe got a sort of idea and picked up the phone.

"So." Tommy bent over to peer more closely. "Who uses Schlege keys?"

"Half of Phoenix." Mel looked pretty bedraggled.

Gretchen wagged her head. "More than half. I've got a Schlege on my front door. And my last apartment, that was a Schlege."

"And he drives a Toyota."

Mel snorted. "So does Gretchen. So do 500,000 other people in Arizona."

Joe punched in the number Sammie had given him. "The third one looks like a locker key. Who would have a locker?"

"Anyone in the police department." Mel looked at Gretchen. "We're rapidly narrowing it down to you, you know."

"Yeah, and I'm frantically trying to think up an alibi."

Joe identified himself to the woman on the line. She transferred him immediately to someone whose name she mentioned so rapidly, Joe couldn't make it out.

A reedy tenor came on. "Phil here. Police?"

"We're trying to find the owner of a ring of keys. You're the local Schlege distributor. I'm hoping you keep records of who purchased what keys."

"We record series. Give me the numbers."

Joe poked at the ring with a pencil. "In larger lettering, M7. And there's a line of smaller lettering." He read it off.

Joe could barely hear a computer keyboard ticking away.

Two minutes later Phil announced, "The city of Phoenix purchased that series. The M7 refers to a submaster."

"So it's a city of Phoenix employee?"

"Right. Just a minute." More ticking. "Works in the central district. Each district has its own submaster."

With thanks and expressions of appreciation, Joe punched that call out and got on the line to the city offices. Four minutes later he ran the locker key down as being issued to one of six names. He had to get spelling on three of them—Kreger, Akihima, and Tanvald. "The other three are Hawkins, Jimenez, and Moreno. It's not a locker. It's a storage shed. They're groundskeepers. Personnel is giving us their home addresses."

Mel's eyebrows rose. "If Aki-whoever is Japanese . . ."

"Akihima," Doug corrected.

". . . and those other two are Hispanic, that leaves us with three Anglos." Mel brightened. "I'll get some uniformed officers on it right now." He swatted Joe's arm. "We'll have that creep scooped up before he realizes he lost his keys."

It sounded easy. Things that sound easy never are, Joe reflected ruefully. Akihima was indeed Japanese. Jimenez and Moreno were most definitely Hispanic. Kreger was fifty-five years old and potbellied. Tanvald's arm was in a cast, the unfortunate result of a fall off his roof.

And Hawkins had given the city personnel office a false address.

Bernice

Joe slipped into a narrow parking space between a Maserati and a Rolls. He could see now why Tom wanted to arrive here in Joe's MG. While his little classic Midget was not in the same price-per-pound class as these other vehicles, it looked a lot snazzier than Tom's kelly green VW bug.

Tom bounced out of the car. "Jose, me lad, I look forward to this. Never been to one of these society garden parties before."

"I've never been hanged for horse-stealing before, either, but that doesn't mean I look forward to it." Joe snapped the tonneau cover and looked around this parking lot carved out of the nearly vertical flank of Camelback Mountain.

"Joe, you're taking the wrong attitude completely. Mrs. Thompson invited us up here to keep an eye on her silver, and I want ye to see her place. A dazzler. If ye don't like hobnobbing with the socialites, look on it as purely a police assignment."

"Yeah." Joe paused beside a rickety, narrow staircase that zigzagged up the steep mountainside and out of sight. "These Camelback mansions are just peachy—if you're a goat."

"Will ye quitcher complaining?" Tom raised a finger. "Hark."

At the far end of the parking lot a little cable car—more like a mine bucket on tracks—came creaking down to a halt. Tom waved a hand toward it. "There we go. Lead on."

Joe stepped into the little car with some trepidation. Tom crowded in beside him, looked around briefly, and tugged on a cotton cord. The car jolted and started grinding straight up the steep cliff. Joe could walk faster than this. On the other hand, the way was too steep in most spots to negotiate. He watched the parking lot get smaller until the scenery stole his full attention. You couldn't fault the view from this little cable bucket. The Salt River Valley stretched out in all directions. They crept precariously up the south face of Camelback Mountain a good 100 feet or more before the car jerked to a stop.

Joe knew perfectly well that some gorgeous homes hugged the side of the mountain and nestled in its crevices, but he'd never seen one like this. The house itself sprawled two stories high and fifty feet deep across a spacious terrace bulldozed into the mountainside. Dark rock with knobby boulders rose directly behind it to frame its white stucco and red Spanish tile. A pale blue pool clung to the edge of the terrace; palm trees thirty feet high lined the cliff behind. Grass, saguaro, bougainvillea, oleander, bamboo, and a host of other exotics splashed color and shades of green everywhere. A gentle scent of incense—jasmine or frangipani—floated across the yard.

Apparently the white-jacketed young man was the hired tram operator. He smiled a greeting as they stepped out of the car. His eye dwelt a moment on Tom's upper lip and his face assumed the most bemused expression. His own dark moustache was thick and full.

At the far end of the yard beneath an arching trellis, the top of a stairway disappeared over the side. No doubt that was the upper terminus of that interminable staircase from the parking lot. A little bell rang. The operator threw a brass lever and the car creaked down out of sight.

"The bell," Joe said. "It rings whenever a car crosses the traffic hose in the parking lot?"

"Yes, sir. I send the car down each time someone drives in."

"Is there a traffic counter on the hose?"

"I don't know, sir."

Tom tugged his sleeve. A woman was crossing the lawn toward them. Joe followed Tom over to meet her.

She was close to fifty and a little plumper than necessary, her hair a little bluer than it should have been, her jewelry a little gaudier than good taste dictated. But the smile was warm, the handshake genuine.

"Mrs. Thompson, I present me partner and best friend, Joe Rodriguez. Joe, Mrs. Whitney Thompson."

"Mr. Rodriguez, I'm delighted you came." Her tone of voice suggested that she was indeed delighted.

"Your servant, Mrs. Thompson." Joe had trouble surveying her jewelry because her face was actually very attractive. She must have been a charming debutante.

She took them both by the hand and led them toward the pool. In the distance Joe saw at least fifty wealthy stereotypes that he did not care to meet. He had to yank his mind back to attention.

Mrs. Thompson was rattling on to Tom. "...about seventy-five people. Not a big party, but not really cozy. The occasion is Whitney's birthday, ostensibly, but he got stuck in Chicago with that airline strike. He won't be in till midnight, I'm afraid."

"At the risk of sounding all business, Mrs. Thompson, might we take a look inside first?" Tom's voice flowed like oil. He was obviously loving this. He should have been born an aristocrat.

"Certainly." She turned toward the house. "We had the collection reappraised recently, with the price of silver altering so drastically, you know." She stopped in the doorway so suddenly Tom almost bumped into her. She turned. "I realize it's polite to tell the guests you're glad they came, but I mean it, especially with you two. Whitney inherited the collection intact. Royce Howard was Whitney's uncle, you know. The house is almost a white elephant—who these days wants a place this big? The silver, though, will be negotiable whether the economy thrives or falters. It's Bernice's future. Her insurance."

"Bernice?"

"She was in Vermont backpacking with her cousins when you were . . . were here, Mr. Flaherty. You didn't meet her."

"Ah, but now ye mention it, I remember ye saying about a daughter."

"Tom told me about your sons," said Joe. Her older boy had died of leukemia and the younger in a freak polo accident.

Her face softened. "That you should remember touches me. That's how I met Mr. Flaherty here, Mr. Rodriguez. He did the investigation and report on Tavery's death. Most gently and tactfully too, I might add."

She led them into the main living room, a vast cavern perfectly decorated in early Spanish. From the corbels on the ceiling beams to the artfully tiled floor, it was picture-perfect, but for one detail. Louvered panels meant to conceal the television set had been pushed aside. Someone in bare feet was watching a Tweety and Sylvester cartoon. The feet dangled idly over the arm of a huge wingback chair.

"Bernice, you should be doing that in your room, dear. We have guests."

"It's a pool party. Let 'em stay out by the pool."

"Bernice . . ." Mrs. Thompson's voice took on a sharp edge.

A head to match the feet flopped backward off the

other chair arm. Tousled red hair billowed out and flowed down the side of the chair. She shot a cursory glance at Tom and stared at Joe. Languidly, the feet swung off the chair arm and the head twisted up and around. She gazed at them with emerald green eyes so deeply hued they had to be contact lenses. Her hair color matched Tom's exactly. She could be anywhere between sixteen and thirty. Joe put her somewhere around twenty-two or twenty-three. The tips of her fingers were cigarette-stained.

She grinned at Tom. "My hair cost me $175. Bet you grew yours for nothing." She looked Joe over as a chimpanzee peels a banana. "Congratulations, Tonto. You've got to be the first Indian Mom's ever invited to one of her little soirees. An equal opportunity breakthrough, if ever I saw one."

Joe didn't look at the mother; it would only have intensified her embarrassment. "You're 25 percent right. Quarter-blood Yaqui. Joe Rodriguez, Miss Thompson, and Tom Flaherty."

"You two aren't here to party, right?" She perched on the chair arm and draped herself across the wingback. In short-short cutoffs and a skimpy, stretchy tube top, she looked absolutely lascivious. "You don't belong, either of you. Something big up?"

"Perhaps . . ."

"Bernice." Mrs. Thompson's voice nearly broke. "Go to your room. This minute."

The girl waved a hand carelessly toward Tom. "If he'll come along up. Nice hair." She peered closely at his lip. "Hope you get over that nasty cold soon. Your lip's all mildewed."

Mrs. Thompson looked like someone recently trampled by a rhinoceros. "She's not usually like this, really. If Whitney were here, she wouldn't act this way. He makes her behave. I can't handle her."

Joe looked at the mother beyond Bernice's head. "Her skin color's good and her pupils are normal. She's not stoned; she's deliberately baiting you."

"Aye," Tom added pleasantly. "Joe's kids try to push the limit every now and again too. He just paddles 'em and they line right up. A little physical education works wonders."

"You have kids?" Bernice wrinkled her nose. "How old?"

"Six and nine—a little older than you seem to be."

Too bad about her disposition. With those eyes and that hair, she could have been the next Julia Roberts. She grinned. "Oh, good. A cut contest! I excel at cut contests, Kemo-sabe."

"Bernice, I forbid you to . . ."

"You go first, Geronimo, any topic. Then I'll come back with something about cheap discount-store shirts. And then you . . ."

"Mrs. Thompson," Tom interrupted. "We've business here and we'd best be at it, aye? And I hope you'll not feel embarrassed on our account. I assure ye we've been dealing with all manner of people for many years, and 'tis easy to see there be no malice in your lass here. We can tell if she's putting on and if she's truly half a bubble off. Your Bernice is only irksome on the outside, and she neither bothers nor embarrasses us."

Joe nodded. "She's just bored. No job?"

"She was laid off last year and had to give up her apartment. With Whitney gone so much, I enjoy having her around." Mrs. Thompson scowled. "Except when there are guests."

Bernice's green eyes flicked from face to face. "You're talking about me as if I were out of state. I'm an adult, you know. I'd appreciate it if you'd quit talking about me behind my back in front of me."

Joe held her eye to eye. "You want to join the big kids? Act like one."

Tom should be handling this—he was the one who could talk a woman into—or out of—anything.

Less than a month before, the department had offered a training course in dysfunctional adults. Kids who are still living at home in their twenties figured prominently. So did "acting out" kids, the gang members and drive-by shootists, but they weren't supposed to still be acting out in their twenties.

The big front door swung open, bringing Arizona brilliance into this cool and quiet room. Tom cleared his throat loudly.

An older black woman had just admitted two more cops, Purley Petersen and Pete Marks.

Pete crossed the room as if he owned the house. "You two can leave now."

Behind Pete, Purley shrugged helplessly and looked pained.

Tom nodded toward the women. "Would you excuse us a moment? Be back directly." Together he and Joe crowded Pete off into a dark corner of the room. Mrs. Thompson instantly hauled her maid into another corner, presumably to discuss the progress of the party outside.

Pete glowered. "I mean it, Rodriguez. Go chase your homicide suspects. We'll take care of our own affairs here."

Joe glanced at Tom.

The Irishman moved in closer. "Purley and we were talking this afternoon, and we . . ."

"I know. The force is split into divisions for a reason. We're here to take care of Mrs. Thompson's silver, so you two can get off it. Your car's parked below."

"Eh now, Pete, tis homicide suspects we be chasing, as ye so colorfully stated it." Tom's voice rolled silky smooth and low. "Mel has Harley and Turk working on the Banks lad's background. Harry Wallace is mucking about in the case up to his elbows. Miguel and Chick and Daisy are snooping into his recent associates, and Henny Nieswonger, bless her heart, has two miles of printouts waiting on our desks. So Joe and I be sniffing out other leads of a homicidal nature."

Pete glared at Joe and Joe had no idea what to say next. "Pete, everyone in the department's working on it one way or another. She was one of us. I don't . . ."

"Get outta here!"

"Bernice!" Mrs. Thompson's gasp carried clear across the vast room. She came running toward them and grabbed at the settee by Tom's elbow. Bernice came popping up as her mother yanked her to her feet.

"I'm sorry, gentlemen! I'm so sorry. I hope she

didn't hear anything she . . ."

Bernice jerked free. "Just at the good part too. I want to see if this big galoot punches Cochise or if . . ."

"You were so right." Mrs. Thompson shuddered. "The counselor who evaluated her says she's not into drugs that he can see, and that she's entitled but not exempt, if that means anything. Personally, I think she needs nothing as much as a good old-fashioned razor strop." She looked directly at Tom. "I mean it. Discipline."

"Harriet," Tom wrapped an avuncular arm across her shoulder, "if that's all she be needing, we'd be delighted to oblige ye. As friends of the family in Whitney's absence, of course."

All this was a bit past Joe. Why did Tom suddenly call her "Harriet"? They were barely acquaintances, and Tom was much too polite—much too Old World—to use her first name. A diversion! That was it, and a beauty too. Get Pete's mind working on other things.

Tom dug a coin out of his pocket and flipped it. "Call it, Jose."

"Nice bluff, boys." The girl looked from face to face.

"Heads."

"You're on, me brawny lad. Heads it be. And give her a lick for me. Meself can't abide redheads with big mouths."

"You don't dare." Bernice looked hard at Joe. A classic wave of panic swept across her face, replaced instantly by a devilish grin. With a cheery whoop, she bolted.

Joe knew she would be quicker than he. He lunged and grabbed but she evaded him. She ran like a rabbit for the door, vaulting the coffee table in her path. Joe jumped the table a stride behind her. She tried to slam the front door in his face as she ran out but he was too close. He yanked it; it whanged open against the doorstop.

She headed out across the patio, bumped into a cocktail waitress and narrowly missed a chaise lounge. She dived into the pool without slowing up, surfaced and flipped like a dolphin around to treading water. Joe screeched to a halt on the pool apron.

Laughing, she spread her arms wide. "Come and get me, Geronimo!"

He glanced around. That was what he was looking for. He opened the door of a low toolshed. He took his time assembling the long aluminum handle, the big nylon pool net. He took more time strolling back to the apron. The whole party was watching intently and feigning disinterest.

Joe braced one foot against the diving board mount. "Come peaceably or come out the hard way."

"Sure thing, Chief Joseph." Her bright grin said she was enjoying this immensely.

He nodded. She was as quick in the water as she was in flight, but he managed to tangle the net over her head on the third pass. He pulled her to the edge, without trying in the least to keep that head above water. He grabbed a handful of thick red hair, gripped her arm. She came out gasping and choking, too waterlogged to curse or fight effectively. And like the trapper who ended up with a skunk in his net, Joe wondered what in heaven's name he was supposed to do next.

"I can just imagine what the people in Internal Affairs would have to say if I actually paddled you, Miss Thompson. So consider yourself chastised." Quickly, when she wasn't expecting it, he scooped his good arm around her, pinning her elbows to her side, and tipped her over. He carried her back to the house under his arm like a sack of beans, as she squirmed and kicked.

Inside the front door, he set her still sputtering on her feet. "My children are growing up without a mother because she died when they were tiny. If you choose not to cherish your mother, that's your problem. But treat her with respect because she *is* your mother." He turned her loose, shoved her away.

She stared at him shaking. She tried to spit but her mouth must have been rinsed dry by the heavily chlorinated water. Even bloodshot, her eyes were beautiful. And no, they weren't contacts. She wheeled and ran away up the stairs. A far door slammed.

He expected Mrs. Thompson to be purple, or at least embarrassed to tears, as he crossed to her. She was smiling. "Thank you, Joe. I'm grateful. If Whitney were here, he would have done exactly that, except that he would have tanned her hide. He doesn't consider twenty-three too old to spank." She turned back to Pete. "As I was saying, you are all my guests. I hope you'll leave behind any differences and just enjoy the afternoon. You two are police officers also, I presume?"

"How churlish of me!" Tom bopped his palm against his forehead. "A thousand apologies! I be pleased to present Pete Marks and Purley Petersen. They're experts in the field of robbery sniffing, the very people to help ye keep your collection. Pete's head of the shebang, and Purley does technical things—piano-moving, haybale-tossing, hippopotamus-lifting. . . ."

Pete was the only one not smiling. He glowered yet at Joe.

"Uh, Harriet?" Joe shifted subjects to keep it moving. "What servants are you employing here full-time now?"

"A cook, the housekeeper, and an accountant on mornings."

"The cook and housekeeper live in?"

"Ginia does . . . the housekeeper. The cook lives out on Hayden Road in a condominium, I believe."

"May we talk to Ginia?"

"Of course. She should be around the kitchen somewhere. I asked her to check on the caterer. Shall I go. . . ?"

Joe raised a hand. "We'll find her. I'm sure Pete and Purley would like a tour of your security system. We'll try not to be too intrusive or put a damper on your party."

"Certainly. Relax and make yourselves comfortable." Mrs. Thompson turned to Pete. "Gentlemen?"

Tom followed Joe out and fell in beside. "That Mrs. Thompson! What a jewel! She had Pete eating out of her hand, she did, the moment she commenced speaking. Proper lady. Quick lady. You realize, me hearty, that Pete's quite right to feel we're treading on his toes."

"We're here on homicide business. That must be Ginia over there, the woman who brought Pete through the door."

"Aye."

"Housekeepers know more about the comings and goings of family members than the families do. I want to know just how much the bored Bernice paints the town and who her buddies are."

"Theft or murder or both?"

"Both." Joe stopped, lest they come too close to listening ears. "Remember the sounds the boy made? B, R, and E?"

"Bernice."

"She no doubt has some very sophisticated recreational activities, and smokes anything that stays lit. If she wants money for the pursuit of pleasure and doesn't want to deal, where might she turn?"

"Aye. Besides, dealing is so gauche. She's strictly upper class."

"Her mother called the silver her future. Maybe Bernice feels she should come into her inheritance a few years early."

"In cahoots with Lawrence. Silences him when he threatens to sell their plans to Pete. But why cut down two people—and one of them innocent?"

"Under the false impression Lawrence had already spilled. Or eliminated the police officer she knew would pursue her."

"Or panicked. Missed Lawrence and hit Mouse. As ye said, 'twas a bad angle."

"I doubt it. According to Mouse the shots came in quick succession; put them both down at once. The murderer probably couldn't have made two clean kills if one were accidental or panic-induced."

Tom wagged his head. "Eh, maybe. Meself doubts Bernice harbors any respect at all for her own dear mother, inheritance, or future."

Joe sighed and started off again, weaving among knots of people. A man in tight scarlet swim trunks and a pot belly walked to the pool edge and fell in, presumably on purpose. The sun was setting, spraying protruding boulders with its warm orange glow. Another young man in a white jacket was lighting tiki torches. Soon 100 of them flared and flickered in the evening breeze.

Joe and Tom talked to Ginia for half an hour. The girl, she said, was twenty-two and certainly no virgin. She often stayed out late, but never for the whole night that Ginia knew of. She was expelled from three private academies and finally graduated from public high school a year late. She was bright enough that she should have gone to college, and she learned quickly when she felt like it. She treated Ginia much better than she treated her own mother, because Ginia refused to take any sass. And yes, up until about a month ago, she boasted of a tall, blond boyfriend named Lawrence.

LITTLE PISTOL

"Excuse me. Are you Detective Rodriguez?"

Joe snapped around in his chair and stood up. "How do you do. Mr. Burnside?"

"Yes. Am I interrupting something? I can return later."

"Not at all. You're interrupting a supplemental report and I'm grateful. I hate filing reports. Be seated. Coffee? Soft drink?"

"No, thank you." Was this Mr. Burnside actually deformed or did he simply hunch over automatically from spending long years at desks? As assistant director of the Heldt Museum, he probably didn't do much besides desk work. He reminded Joe of a Dickens character, but which one?

"I appreciate your taking time to drop by." Joe plunked down in his chair again.

"Not at all," Otis Burnside perched like an injured bird on the edge of his, "since I had business downtown here anyway. Sixth and Adams, right around the corner. We agreed it would be easiest for all if I stopped in."

"We?"

"Mrs. Schumacher and I."

"Ah yes, the director. All the same, your time is valuable. I'll try to be brief." Joe didn't mention that brevity was being forced on him; there was only about half an hour left on his tape recorder. He hit the button surreptitiously as he rummaged for a notebook. "You're the assistant director, and your particular forte is Indian silver work?"

"Yes. Your warning about a possible theft came as a shock. I suppose we always think, 'It can't happen here.' We intensified security measures, anticipating trouble. We're grateful for your tip-off."

"As an adjunct of your job, you're familiar with some of the private collections in the valley, right?"

"Very much so. I've appraised most of them at one time or another. Insurance company requirements, you know. It's a service of the museum. We do them at cost. Our appraisals are authoritative."

"I can believe it. Do your appraisals mention or evaluate the private security systems? Burglar alarms and such?"

"No. The art objects only." He fidgeted a bit and shifted in his chair. "The insurance companies take the security system into close consideration, but that's between them and the individuals. I am not an authority on security."

"Sure I can't get you something? Drink dispenser

right over there."

"Thank you. I'm fine." He looked anything but fine. "May I ask a question?"

"Certainly."

"This is apparently the homicide division, but you seem primarily interested in robbery . . ."

"Interdepartmental cooperation. We're working on a case that heavily involves both divisions. Routine, actually."

"Mmm." Mr. Burnside looked doubtful.

Joe switched topics quickly. "Beautiful ring. Wedding band?"

"Thank you, yes. My wife's matches it, of course. We had them made by a Hopi up on the mesas. I met the man at the museum's first craft fair. That was fourteen years ago." He extended his hand to Joe for a better look. Exquisitely worked swirls of turquoise chips braided themselves through a silver matrix.

"You have a craft fair coming up in September, I hear."

"Fifteenth annual. Indian arts and crafts. Outstanding artists. Yes."

Joe sat back, planning where to go. "If you were rating private collections in Arizona, which would you put at the top of the list? Most valuable, splashiest, most important?"

He thought a moment. "I'm not sure I should divulge that. An appraisal is confidential."

"Not as an appraiser. Not just collections you've touched professionally. I have no idea which collections you've appraised personally. As a private citizen, a man who loves fine silver work for its own sake."

"Ah. Fred Harvey collection. I'd rate that tops."

"By what criteria?"

"Several. Extent of the collection. A grouping containing only contemporary pieces is of less value than one representing a broad range of styles and periods. The degree of skill in the handwork. And the kind of turquoise, the way it's used in a piece, affects the value tremendously. Bisbee turquoise, for example, would be much higher in value both artistically and monetarily, than, say...."

Joe listened with one ear as he studied Mr. Burnside. The Dickens character popped out—Uriah Heep. This man was Uriah Heep incarnate. Joe wished Tom were here. Tom not only got to the points he wanted faster, but he had a way of channeling such endless monologues into something useful. Mr. Burnside's phrasing and especially his flat tone of voice were terribly tiresome.

Joe got the man back on track. "Here in the valley, whose would you rate highly?"

"The Andrews Auto collection. Andrews dealership on Grand Avenue. Not just silver, either. Pottery, baskets, kachinas, Western art. And our own, of course. The Heldt collection is second to none. Better than the Museum of Northern Arizona, if I do say so."

"Carver Cadillac?"

He shook his head. "Too modern. All contemporary."

"I understand your Heldt collection is like an iceberg—90 percent in the vault, 10 percent visible on display."

Mr. Burnside diddled his fingers, twirling his

wedding ring. "True. We display only a few representative pieces of each style and period."

"Not necessarily the most expensive?"

"That's right. In fact, some of the most valuable pieces are not, for museum purposes, worth displaying." His fidgeting was becoming a rapid, uncontrolled flutter.

"Who determines which pieces languish in the vault and which go on display?"

Burnside licked his lips. "Mrs. Schumacher has the final say, of course, but she leaves it to my judgment."

"How does Heldt obtain silverwork?"

"We try to maintain a budget for acquisitions, but it usually gets gobbled up by other things. Donations mostly. Yes. Donations."

"Tax write-offs?"

"Until the law changed. We still get occasional gifts, usually from estates of the deceased; executors who want a small collection kept intact, for example."

"On those rare occasions when you purchase a piece, how do you ensure that it hasn't been stolen?"

"We never take stolen goods."

"Of course not. But how do you make sure?"

His rapid flutter had become wild flapping. His hands danced. "Various ways. Most people engrave an inconspicuous mark or their social security number on each piece. Often a private mark."

"And you can trace a piece's history from that?"

"Usually. And whereas the pieces may look alike to most people, there are distinctives—the manner in which the elements are formed..."

"Squash blossoms, beads, and such?"

"Yes. The naja, that is, the big medallion or centerpiece that hangs down the very front of a necklace. The way the turquoise, if any, is set. The origin of the turquoise and its exact color; same thing for coral if it's present. The fineness of the silver. Many ways to describe a piece as being unique, or nearly so."

"Once an engraved mark is on a piece, it's there forever?"

Mr. Burnside had lost control of his hands. Now his feet were starting to vibrate. "It can be removed with difficulty. You must know how. An expert could, but... excuse me." He fished through his pockets. His quivering fingers nearly dropped the little phial of pills. Joe wanted to reach out and help him as he shook a pill out. It looked like a downer of some sort, but Joe couldn't really tell and he couldn't read the prescription label.

Uriah smiled apologetically. "A chronic nervous condition." He popped the pill and sat there staring past Joe, his body rigid and his hands doing jigs in his lap. The jigs abated.

"Other top-notch collections?"

"Many. Goldborough. Jessup Galleries. Navajo Co-op. Hubbell. Mrs. Humboldt here in town. Mrs. Wilton is getting there, if her husband keeps buying her silver as he has been."

"You didn't mention Royce Howard."

"That too. Some inferior pieces, but overall a nice collection. Not as well rounded as I would like to see, but nice." His hands were dancing again in spite of the medication. He pulled a pocket watch and glanced at it. It was one of those ornate and heavy railroad watches. "I should be getting on. Perhaps I can stop in again another day, if you need more."

"One last quick question. What can you tell me about a young man named Lawrence Banks?"

"I don't recall ever hearing that name."

"Tall, good-looking, about twenty-five, blond beard."

Nothing in the man's face suggested he was anything but truthful as he said, "No, I don't think I ever met him."

Joe stood up. "Thank you very much for your cooperation, Mr. Burnside. Tom and I would like to stop by Heldt in the next day or so, if we may." He extended his hand.

Joe routinely took a person's right hand with his right, then closed the left down over both for the squeeze, since he had no grip to speak of in his right hand. But Otis Burnside had no squeeze at all. He shook with a clammy semiclasp, mumbled some polite things, and scurried out, crablike. Uriah Heep.

"Now that's an interesting mix for you." Gretchen's voice startled him. Joe turned. She perched on the corner of his desk swinging one foot. Gretchen Wiemer had the longest legs of any woman (and most of the men) on the force.

He plopped back into his chair. "How's that?"

"He looks like a minimum-wage bank clerk, but he's wearing a $600 suit."

Joe frowned. "Oh, yeah? Didn't notice. Hung like

a basset's jowls on him."

"On him, a $1,000 suit would. Here's the data so far on Mouse. Doug and you pulled off the coup of the week. Y'know that smudge you pointed out? Where you thought someone might have been hanging out the window?"

"It was actually made by a disoriented bat that missed its way."

"Close. It was made by a shootist less than five-foot-nine. Doug did some infrared, photomicros, powder test; even got a partial print. Brilliant piece of forensic wizardry based on your observation."

"That'll narrow the field of suspects, soon as we get any."

"Got your supplementals done yet? Pete Marks especially wants a transcript of your conversation with Mouse."

"I want him to get the one concerning Thompsons too. Otis Burnside interrupted. Fifteen minutes. Hang around, if you're taking deliveries."

"Tommy coming in soon?"

"Maybe."

"I'll chance it. Type on." She slid off the desk and carelessly cast herself into Tom's chair.

Joe had pecked out maybe a dozen words when another female voice startled him.

"Planning your social calendar? Any good cotillions this month?" Bernice perched herself on the desk corner Gretchen had so recently vacated. A temporary visitor card was tucked in the waistband of her shorts; Joe wondered what Grace Red Morning, out on the desk, thought about that. Grace was quite modest. Bernice carried the morning paper and a stack of library books. She dropped the books on his desk *clunk.*

Joe glanced at Gretchen. She was trying to hide a smug little grin. He nodded at her. "Miss Thompson. Good morning."

She shook the paper open. "You made the big time, Kemo-sabe. Sonja Sachs' column. That's hotter than the social register." She folded the paper appropriately and thrust it at him. She twisted to look at Gretchen. "Are you his appointment or his date?"

"Do you know what *paramour* means, little girl?"

"Yeah."

"Well, I ain't one. Just checking to see if you knew."

Bernice turned her green eyes back to Joe. "You run with a whole herd of sharpies. Tom Flaherty, and this cookie . . ."

Gretchen asked, "Tom knows this chick?"

"Bosom buddies." Joe scanned the column without absorbing every word. Among the social notes was a three-sentence paragraph about how Joe Rodriges (misspelled) had flirtatiously chased Whitney Thompson's daughter into the pool at a party. The phrasing was snide, the innuendo clear: lowly minority folk who drink copiously should not attend upper-class parties.

He handed the paper back to her. "Only thing Miss Sachs failed to mention was that you deserved it. You still do."

She opened her mouth to speak, no doubt to offer some snide retort, when her eye caught the book describing dog breeds on Joe's desk. She picked it up, thumbed through it and grinned. "Scoping possible dates?"

"You were right. You are very good at cuts. The kids want a dog, so we're looking at different breeds."

She tossed the book aside. "One of the things Mom likes best about our house is there's no neighbor dogs to poop on our lawn. I guess that used to be a problem when we lived on Lafayette. How come Mr. Burnside was in a police station?"

"You know Otis Burnside?"

"No, I just picked the name out of a lottery basket this little Mexican girl was toting around in the hallway."

"You passed him in the hall as you were coming up and he was going out."

"Very shrewd. You mean he was right here with little old you?" Her eyes were gorgeous.

"Best seat in the house, right here. How do you know him?"

"He did an insurance fudge on the jewelry and flatware for us. He made a pass at me once, when we were alone in the same room, so I gave him a fat lip." She crossed her legs.

"What did he say when he saw you coming in here?"

"Why'd you ask that?"

"Officers of the law ask all kinds of dumb stuff."

"He didn't say anything. But he stopped cold and stared at me like I was Godzilla. His eyes even got real wide. Then he scurried off to his hole, I guess. You see how he moves. Hunched. Weird."

"If he were tall, dark, and handsome, would he

have gotten a fat lip?"

"Want to try and see for yourself? You happen to be two out of three, and that ain't bad. I can live without the tall."

"Naw. Not that cops don't make passes now and then." He leaned forward suddenly, grabbed her pile of library books and scooped them into his lap to be examined at leisure. Two were junk romance novels, one a current best-seller about a torrid and tragic *ménage à trois,* and the other two were detailed treatises on human physiology. "Is Otis Burnside a family friend, a silver assayer only, or what?"

"He doesn't play golf or tennis or go swimming, so my father doesn't associate with him. Mom invited him up once or twice just to be sociable, because he did the appraisals for free. He knows George. That's about it. You know, the way you ask questions sounds kind of like those TV cops."

"They're all pallid imitations of me. George Who?"

"I dunno."

"George What?" Joe divided his attention between the conversation and the flap copy on the back of one of the romance novels.

"George the Gardener. Comes in a couple times a week to tend the grounds. Fetid breath, crooked teeth, yellow eyes, stupid. Other than that, a sterling individual."

"What's the connection between Burnside and this George? A museum director and a lowly gardener? You know?"

"Who cares? I just came by to let you see your name in print, Tecumseh."

He took the paper back again, shook it open and refolded it to the front page. "I already have my name in print—spelled correctly too. Investigating officer; indirect quote in the third paragraph there." He tapped the page. "The girl labeled 'slain cop' was nicknamed Mighty Mouse around here. She had as many brains as you do, but I doubt she had more than you. She put them to good use and made the most of her God-given talents. Too bad you never met her. She's a great role model for bored young women with plenty of savvy and no ambition."

She gathered up her books, balanced the paper on them and studied it a moment. With a grin she hopped off her perch and dropped the paper in his lap. "Perfect little daughter any mother would be proud to claim." She pointed to the picture on page one. "See what it got her? Toodle-oo." She flounced out.

Gretchen stared after her. "Any comment I made would be anticlimactic." She glanced over at Joe and gaped. "But she got to you! That little pistol really got to you! Paternal or prurient?"

"I don't know." Joe watched the door through which Bernice had just disappeared. The name fit. The size fit. The devil-be-hanged attitude fit just fine. Then again, with Bernice, nothing really fit. "I don't know."

Pawn Peddler

"Sauerkraut?" Tom stood at the Wienie Barn window slopping catsup across his hot dogs. He passed the dispenser to Joe.

"No thanks. Put much more on those things and you'll need a winch to lift them." He slurped catsup over his own two dogs.

"A weiner without trimmings is like a circus without elephants. A zoo without camels. A beer wagon without horses." Tom glanced at him sideways. "A cop without a ready line of patter. Tell me what be bothering ye. You're as noisy as a mouse in house slippers."

"That gastric catastrophe you call lunch, for starters. Sauerkraut *and* chili?" Joe picked one of those little circular outdoor tables in a far corner of the ramada.

Tom plunked down across from him and thrust a

straw into his drink. "Ye forget how well I know ye. Beneath that heart of gold lies a stomach of iron. Me lunch doesn't bother ye. Business or Bernice?" Tom did that constantly, put a precise finger on Joe's thoughts.

Even so, every time he did it caught Joe unprepared. "Both. They may be one and the same. Bernice is cold enough to ice two people and never suffer a moment of remorse."

"I doubt it, but that's just me instincts speaking, not me observations. She fits the bill so far, including alibi. For the time in question she has none. Claims to've been at the library."

"Check any materials out?"

"No, and it would've been handy. We could've pinpointed within an hour that her library card, at least, had been there. Incidentally, I can't find a last name for this Lawrence ex-boyfriend of hers. She claims she doesn't know it herself; what they call a casual relationship, I believe. Is me question answered?"

"Which question?"

"About what's bothering ye."

"Why no make on the fingerprints on the keys? The guy has to have a police record hanging around somewhere."

"True. People so wary of the law that they run away at the sight of one of its practitioners usually have a yellow sheet long enough to hide behind without stooping over. He does not fit the pattern."

"Right. And there's the shavings."

"Aye, the shavings. In Gretchen's supplemental on the lad's clothing. Not sawdust, she says, but too small to come from a carpenter's shop. Ragged splinters."

Joe paused long enough to finish a hot dog. "According to Harry, this Banks never worked in construction or carpentry or anything that would put wood particles in his clothes."

"No hobbies, either. Like woodworking, or ship models. Turk worked on that angle."

Halfway through the second hot dog a light dawned. "Tommy, he does indeed have a hobby to account for it. Let's go see Pete Marks when we're done here."

An hour later in the claustrophobic confines of Robbery, Pete Marks, sullen as ever, surveyed his fiefdom from a leaning position near the water cooler. He talked to Joe without looking at him. "Couple minor jobs this week. Nothing much. Always slow in summer."

"Any silver?" Joe scanned the huddled desks, the ticking terminals, the telephone conversants.

"Now and then. Look, I don't handle the individual investigations. You know that. I don't know every little hot item."

Tom's voice cooed, "Let me rephrase our request. We'd like to see your files of recent jobs, last couple days."

Pete glared at him. "You two are Homicide, remember?"

"Aye, well enough. We're trying to find connections to this Lawrence Banks. He's from out of town; no friends locally; ye saw Harley and Turk's summaries. Moved three times in four months. We can't get a solid hold on him."

"So?"

"Ye read the lab report."

"Still, so?"

"Might the wood splinters mentioned therein not come from a burglary, since burglary be one of his favorite sports? Maybe jimmying one of those old style wood-sash windows or the like?"

"Suppose it could. Pretty thin."

"When that's the only straw to snatch at, ye grab for it."

"So why ask me? The files are available to any qualified personnel."

"Because ye run the division." Tom's voice drifted smooth and gentle as smoke. Joe envied Tom's gift for expressive yet subtle voice inflections.

Pete wandered off across the room and swatted a drawer. "Hard copies in here. Don't mess 'em up." He walked away.

Joe watched Pete disappear out the double doors. Tom yanked the drawer open and started riffling. He handed Joe three folders and shuffled through a handful for himself. Purley appeared beyond Tom and leaned on the cabinet watching. The cabinet groaned.

"Jose, me lad, you're a genius! I do believe 'tis here. Perfect date too; the very night before the lad died."

Joe abandoned his own folders to peer over Tom's shoulder.

Tom was absolutely glowing. "Cinder-block house built in the '50s. Wood frame windows. The burglar chewed up the kitchen window getting in, pictures enclosed. Took—let's see—took gold flatware service for eight; jewelry, partial inventory attached; silver tea service—three pieces; and two six-packs of beer."

"Jewelry." Joe reached across Tom's arm and lifted a page to see the partial inventory. "Usual stuff, and $3,000 in Navajo silver."

Purley craned his neck around to look. "Is that Fletcher's booze-and-bear fetish?"

Joe frowned. "The inventory lists a necklace with a bear-shaped naja."

Tom flipped back to the front page. "Aye, Bob Fletcher's."

Purley nodded. "Then I have an update for you. We found the necklace and a few other pieces in a pawnshop. Picked up the shop owner for possession of stolen goods and couldn't keep him. He's a suspected fence, but we've never been able to nail him."

"No culprit?"

"Not yet."

"Ah, then we've an update for yourself, though we'll have to confirm it with a little lab work—paint and wood samples. Lawrence Banks."

"Not *the* Lawrence Banks!"

"The one and only. Who's the fence?" Joe corrected himself. "Alleged fence?"

"Fellow runs a side-by-side used furniture store and pawnshop. Name John Berendsi. We musta spent 200 hours on him and he's still in business."

"Berendsi. Five-foot-eight or less?"

"Just about an even five-eight. Dumpy build. Hey, I heard about Doug Hakamura's little coup there." Burl launched his bulk to perpendicular and rubbed his hands together. "Talk about your basic redneck. His general attitude makes the Klan look like the ACLU. Do I get to go along?"

"Of course, me daughty chum." Tom stuffed the files back in the drawer. "The more the merrier."

Berendsi. Burnside. Bernice. Joe could imagine the topic of his next nightmare—a telephone directory of nothing but Bs.

Neither Joe's car nor Tom's would carry three grown men when one of them was Burly Purley, so they took Purley's squad car. The whole lackluster neighborhood around the pawnshop, mostly older storefronts and cheap single-story homes, seemed deserted; but in summer a lot of Phoenix looks deserted.

Joe climbed out of the car and looked up at the flaked and fading store sign. "Wonder what ever happened to the three hanging globes that marked pawnshops. Remember them?"

"Aye," sighed Tom. "Went the way of dodos and house calls, no doubt."

"As I recall, this shop used to have one of those things years ago," said Purley. "Kids with BB guns and 22s shot the globes out all the time. Guess he got tired of replacing them."

"Ye grew up here, aye?"

"Not quite a native." Purley grinned. "My folks moved here when I was three. Population was half a million then."

"And the population of the whole state of Arizona was less than a million. I remember." Joe nodded. A little bell went ding as he glanced up at the street sign on the corner.

"Aaah, me chaps, now ye make me feel like a foreigner."

"Aintcha?" Purley looked at him.

Tom wagged his head. "The pity of it. There be Mexican-Americans, Swedish-Americans, German-Americans, Armenian-Americans, but only Irishmen-in-America." Tom turned to watch Joe. "What're ye doing?"

Joe waved a hand to shush him, because Henrietta's voice on the patch-through was kind of murky. "Yeah. Tom just pulled them. The traffic violations."

Tom hung on the door. "Begorra! The lad's parking ticket!"

Purley crowded in closer. "There were four locations, but I forget which one was the night before Teacher dismissed him."

"Thanks, Hennie. Thanks very much." Joe hung up the mike. "Gentlemen, we are sitting on the exact spot where Lawrence Banks earned his final parking ticket."

Tom stood erect. "Now all sorts of delightful questions raise their lovely heads. Which angle do we use? Suggestions?"

Joe stared at Purley a moment. No answers there. "Play it by ear, I suppose." He stood up and locked the car door.

The interior door connecting the pawnshop with the furniture store stood open at a casual tilt. It probably neither opened nor closed all the way. Both shops were dark and musty, and cried out for the services of a cleaning lady. Joe glanced through the door into the furniture store as they entered the pawnshop. Furniture pieces were stacked and stored without regard to form or function. Everything needed refinishing.

Here in the pawnshop, a listless black girl slouched on a stool behind the counter. Only when she saw Purley did she show any sign of life. "You again, huh?"

"Tom and Joe, this is Lu Ella Parkins. John couldn't get along without her."

"Hi." The huge dark eyes flicked distrustfully from face to face and then rested on Purley. "You gonna arrest him again?"

Purley shrugged. "So far, we're just here to talk. He in the back room there?"

She nodded. Joe smiled and gave her a "Nice to meet you" as Tom offered cheery words of greeting. They followed Purley to the back and left Lu Ella on her perch with nothing to do.

The office, such as it was, was hardly bigger than a file cabinet, but it held three of them. All three were so overfilled with files the drawers didn't close completely. Berendsi, a dumpy, sullen, balding man, looked too fat to be able to squeeze between the cabinets and his cluttered desk and the cardboard cartons and the stacks of papers. For sure his tilting desk chair didn't have room to tilt back all the way. The place was a trash bin.

Purley waved a hand. "John Berendsi here is another of my many admirers. Joe and Tom, John Berendsi."

Berendsi scowled at them. "I thought you said you were done with me, Petersen."

Joe squeezed in and closed the office door behind

him, although Lu Ella didn't look like an eavesdropper. She sat on her stool with a vacant stare.

"That bear-naja necklace, John. You claim you don't remember who brought it in." Purley fit in this closet worse than Joe did.

"Still don't."

"So we're here to fill you in. It was lifted by a young man named Lawrence Banks who..."

"Never heard of him."

Tom chimed in. "Ah now, Johnny, me lad, don't give us that. Ye did occasional fencing for our Lawrence Banks until his untimely demise. Ye know it and we know it. So let's start from there, aye?"

"What are you? Some kind of foreigner?"

Tom wagged his head at Joe. "Ye see? Makes me point."

Joe got a grand notion—well, at least the germ of an idea worth pursuing. "Mr. Berendsi, you say you've never heard of this Lawrence Banks. I have no reason not to believe you. Purley, did you find anything at all linking this man with Banks? Besides the jewelry, I mean."

"Not directly. No."

Joe nodded. "Then it's got to be that clerk out there. Tommy, what say we take her downtown?" He swung the door open and headed out into the shop.

"Sounds good to me." Tom followed him.

Berendsi exploded behind them. "Wait a minute!" Boxes clunked and cabinets clanged as he fought his way to the door.

Joe marched smartly to the front counter. "Get your purse, please, miss. You're coming with us."

Her eyes flipped open wider than wide. "Me? *Me??!*"

Purley picked the ball up and carried it smoothly. "Yes, Lu Ella. You were on the premises here when stolen goods were recovered. We have hard evidence that Lawrence Banks is the thief. And we have hard evidence that Banks was here the night of the theft. Your job is a perfect cover for fencing."

"Not me! No sirree! I swear I don't know nothin' 'bout no stolen goods."

"We'll talk about it downtown." Purley grabbed an elbow and steered her toward the door. Tom ran interference, darting ahead.

Berendsi ducked to the side in both directions and still couldn't get around Joe. "You can't just take her like that! I need her here. And she doesn't have anything to say without a lawyer around. And she doesn't talk unless I'm present!"

"Oh?" Joe raised his eyebrows. "You a member of the bar?"

"I don't hafta be. I know . . ."

"A member of the family, perhaps. Father or brother?"

"Don't get wise with me, you spick!"

"Then butt out. We'll let you know if we decide to keep her overnight, so you can arrange her bail. Or find someone else to tend the cash register."

Berendsi pushed past him and charged out the door. The girl was looking wildly, helplessly at Berendsi as Purley stuffed her into the backseat.

Berendsi shouted, "You keep your black mouth shut, you hear? You don't tell 'em nothing! I'll be down soon as I close up." He wheeled and bumped into Joe. Livid, he shoved past angrily and disappeared into the gloom of his store.

The door slammed.

Spick, huh? Some busts are more fun than others.

Lu Ella Sings

Lu Ella Parkins wasn't exactly fat, but she was stocky enough that you knew she'd be a very heavy woman in her later years. She and Tom were an interesting study in contrasts—her thick build with Tom Flaherty's lanky leanness; her black skin and Tom's coloring so fair he was more pink than white; her hair done in tight cornrows and his unruly orange bush in perpetual need of grooming. She sat at the dull gray table in the only cubicle available at the moment, and Tom had parked himself not across from her, lest the table form a barrier, but at her left.

Purley and Joe were across the hall in a room almost as dismal, sipping at cold soft drinks and watching Tom and Lu Ella, courtesy of the closed circuit TV. It wasn't exactly "Donahue," but it was certainly more immediately relevant.

"How old are ye, Miss Parkins?"

"Nineteen, almost twenty. You know that Petersen detective already asked me all this stuff."

"Now don't be taking all the fun out of me job here, I beg ye. You've a warm, rich voice and meself enjoys hearing it. A rare pleasure in this business, finding someone ye like listening to. Live at home?"

"No. Live over the store."

"With John."

"Mmm hmm."

"Don't ye ever get sick of him putting ye down because of your color, lass?"

"Don't everybody?"

Tom chuckled. "There ye have me, lass. Again, Miss Parkins, be ye sure ye don't want a lawyer present here?"

"Ain't gonna get stuck for no lawyer, no."

"Tis a service of the house. No charge. Free."

"Nothing's free. Every time something's free, I get stuck. No."

"As ye wish. Miss Parkins, uh . . . might I call ye Lu Ella? Lu Ella's a lovely name and 'Miss Parkins' sounds so cold."

She shrugged.

"And if ye would, just to keep things even, call me Tom."

She studied him for a moment. "Growing a moustache?"

"Aye," Tom purred.

"Looks like a woolly-bear caterpillar with summer mange."

"Ah, well, give it time. Just commenced." Tom

shifted in his chair and started off with the basic questions, touching on personal and peripheral things.

The phone beside Joe made him jump. He picked it up.

"Rodriguez."

"What are *you* doing over there, slumming? Got some stuff here Purley Petersen wants." Hennie Nieswonger, the maven of records, sounded like a tough old logger. In person, she looked like one.

Purley glanced at Joe. "Is it Hennie? You take it." He turned his attention back to the closed-circuit monitor.

"He says it's all mine."

"Ain't he generous." Henrietta droned in monotone, "Never owned a vehicle. Got in official trouble twice, both times for prostitution. First case dropped, second suspended. Got through tenth grade and part of the eleventh. Classed as marginal MR. No hits nationally."

"Thanks, Hennie. Send a printout to the Burl, eh?"

"Even threw in a cross-check for aliases. Zip."

"You're a jewel among keypunch operators. We appreciate it."

"Keypunch?! I'm an *artiste,* Rodriguez, and don't you forget it."

"Thanks, Rembrandt." Joe cradled it. "Tagged for public relations twice, no action. Semi MR. Clean."

Purley nodded sagely. "Nothing new since the last time I ran her through. Kinda hoping for an increase in IQ. She didn't sound like a kid out to make a quick buck when I talked to her the first time. Still doesn't. Look at that Irishman work. He's skating circles all around her."

Tom was leaning so far back he was practically off the screen. "Then you'd say, Lu Ella, that Berendsi or any other pawn dealer could be trading in hot items now and then?"

"No way you can check real close."

Tom paused, groping through pockets for his cigarettes. He found a pack and shook it out—two left. He extended the pack toward her and she grabbed one without hesitating.

"Thanks." She leaned forward for a light.

"During store hours, ye accept goodies and pay out money?"

"Sometimes. If it's something I know the value of."

"How about after hours? Anyone bring stuff in after hours?"

"When we closed, we closed."

He nodded and lit his own.

She scowled at her cigarette. "What brand is this? Tastes terrible!"

"Hard to get, this brand. Tis an acquired taste, like olives." Tom leaned back again, as far from her as he could manage. "Picture this scene, Lu Ella. Tis about eleven o'clock at night. A tall, blond, bearded young man comes in, up the back stairs. He pounds on the door and John lets him in."

Her eyes, half closed a moment before, opened.

"The lad has quite a bundle. Pretty things. Gold flatware, a lovely tea set—ye know, pot and sugar and creamer—some nice jewelry. The necklace especially, with the bear on it. John buys it, but they get into a howling argument. Now what do ye care to add to me picture?"

"No way you can know all that!"

"Then how do I? Ask yourself that."

"I don' know . . ."

"Well, pause and think it through. I could be making it all up in me head, but I couldn't imagine all those true details. Or I could've heard about it from the blond chap. Ye know, he was the one killed the very next morning, along with that young lady police officer. Or else, John himself told me. Did ye read the piece in the paper about the lad? The shooting?"

She shook her head. "Saw some of it on the TV. The announcer said he didn't say nothing 'fore he died."

"That's right, which lets him out. So either I made it all up, or John told us."

"Then you musta guessed it. John wouldn't tell nothin'."

"Kind of hard, lass, to describe the scene so perfectly if I be guessing, eh?" Tom leaned forward and put a sincere tone of earnestness in his voice. ". . . unless John thinks we're getting too close. Mayhap he even thinks we might be planning to tack the murders on him. He could be setting yourself up to take the rap."

Her eyes were approaching golf-ball size.

Tom crooned on. "For a fact ye know he denies things that are true. He's a first-class liar, well practiced. And he's not got that high an opinion of ye, the gruff way he's always talking to ye. I don't think he loves ye, lass."

"I know he don't. And I don't love him. He's regular meals, that's all. It's a job, and I can't find a job easy."

She was cracking wide open but Tom withdrew his wedge. He darted off to other things, planting further subtle suspicions, making subliminal assurances.

Purley poked Joe. "Where'd he get that scenario?"

"Fertile imagination. A combination of that parking ticket that put Banks there and the time, Fletcher's inventory of the stolen items, the supposition that a redneck bigot like Berendsi couldn't help but pick a fight with anyone in a beard. He's a genius."

"Ain't he though!"

Tom pulled his chair in close now; comforting, fatherly. His voice dropped. "You're not a bad lass, Lu Ella. The more I talk to ye, the better I like ye. Ye don't deserve to be dumped on by the likes of John Berendsi. I don't want to see it happen." His voice dropped further. "The best way ye can protect yourself is simply to tell the truth. In 99 cases out of 100 if everyone just told the simple truth, they would never have seen trouble. We don't want ye to fink on John, neither to protect him. Just let the truth have its own way."

Hard by Joe's elbow, the phone rang again. "Hang! Right at the good part too. Rodriguez."

"Benny on the front desk, Joe. A Mr. Berendsi is here, fussing and fuming, to see Purley Petersen."

"Benny down front, Burl. One of your many admirers."

"I ain't home."

"He ain't home. That's his phrasing, not mine."

Benny's voice hesitated. "Tell him 'later'?"

"If at all. Mr. Petersen is in conference and unavailable. Thanks, Benny." He hung up.

On the screen Tom was returning to the scenario he had set up. "John knew Lawrence Banks had stolen the items he brought. He'd know that from the hour, even if they'd never dealt before. But Lawrence Banks did deal with him, and regularly. True?"

"Yeah."

"And now this time. Gorgeous stuff too. How much did John give the lad for all that?"

"The usual."

"What's usual? Ten cents on the dollar?"

"Five. He offered him $135 for the bag."

"Naturally Banks protested the sum was far too low."

"Ever'body does. So John upped it to $150 even."

"And Banks says, so to speak, 'You're spitting in me eye.' Did he take the $150?"

"What did John say? Did John tell you he took it?"

"Lass, I don't believe a word of what John says. He'd say young Banks took it with humble gratitude, whether it happened or not. He'd never admit to cheating the lad."

"Yeah, you're right. He won't admit he cheats me, but I know he does. I know it, but I can't prove it."

"And ye doubt he'd turn ye in to save his own hide? Tell me about the argument between them.

Just the truth."

"Loop said he'd take the things somewhere else before he'd sell 'em that cheap. And John said he didn't need Loop's stuff."

"Loop? Lawrence Banks?"

"They call him Loop. Dunno why. John said he was coming into a real big haul and didn't need Loop. Big haul."

"Museum quality silver work?"

"You know, expensive stuff." She thought a moment. "Don't remember any museum."

"Silver and turquoise, though?"

She pumped her head up and down. "I don't remember the argument exactly because I hid in the other room. When John gets mad at someone, he usually takes it out on me."

"Then Loop threatened to tell the police about John's big haul, aye?"

"Yeah. John said he didn't dare. Loop said he did too. I don't remember who won."

Tom wagged his head sadly. "And ye know, Lu Ella, John never said a word to us about any argument, any fight with Loop, and that's the truth. Not a blinking word did he say about it."

"He's real sneaky, I know that much." She looked at her cigarette again. "These things aren't so bad once you get used to them."

"The next day after the fight there, was Berendsi in the store all day?"

"I don' know. He comes and goes, parks his car out back. I just sit on the register when the place is open. And Mrs. Cutter, she takes the furniture store on Saturdays."

"So ye don't know when he's in and when he's not."

She shook her head and ground the cigarette butt into the ashtray.

Tom patted her hand. "Lu Ella, I'll never breathe a word of our conversation, lest John cause ye grief. He'll no doubt ask ye what we talked about here. Ye can tell him we no longer consider ye a prime suspect, and ye needn't mention anything else. Tell him it was confidential but harmless."

Joe looked at Purley. "Would Berendsi have any compunctions about hurting her?"

"None that I can see. Since he's on our doorstep anyway—"

The door in the next room exploded open. Pete Marks appeared on screen. Lu Ella popped to her feet and Tom jumped two inches.

Pete roared, "Where's Purley?!"

Tom nodded across the hall and disguised the motion as a cock of the head. "Had other business to attend, he said."

"Go home, Flaherty!" Pete stepped back and slammed the door.

Joe and Purley looked at each other and braced. The door whanged open. Pete was livid. "That's your robbery suspect! How come you're sitting here like a nerd while that Irishman works on her?"

Purley stood up. "What is this, anyway, Pete? You don't. . . ."

"Rodriguez, I'm telling you for the last time. Go mind your own store or I start making phone calls."

The back of his neck prickled, as much from anger as anything. Joe forced a smile and spread his hands wide. "See you later, Pete. Purley, explain to him about the parking ticket and the bear necklace, and tell Tom I'm out in the lobby. Might even bump into one of your many admirers." He left.

He had told himself a dozen times that he'd take it easy with Pete, at least while Mouse's loss was still so painfully fresh. His noble conviction was a royal pain in the patoot. One of these times he was going to rain all over Pete before he could stop himself.

He found Berendsi at the far end of the lobby, ready to spit nails. The man's temper matched his spare tire and perhaps exceeded it. Was Berendsi a man who vented his spleen immediately? Or would he let it simmer—stalk and kill in cold blood?

The only positive result Joe achieved in ten minutes of confronting the pawnbroker was to assure the man that if Lu Ella Parkins were injured in any way, dark thugs with foreign-sounding names would fall upon Berendsi in the dead of night.

Dog Gone

Doom and despair. Joe absolutely dreaded this morning.

"This is exciting!" Nine-year-old Rico bounced into his seat at the rear of the Suburban and belted himself in.

"Yeah!" In the middle seat, six-year-old Glo tugged her seat belt down tight.

"Mahhh-ahhm!" Rudy whined. "I get the window seat this time."

Glo glared across at him. "No you don't! Aunt Fel. . . ?"

"You had it last time, Rudy." Joe's sister Fel sat in the front passenger seat looking as grim as Joe felt.

"Everybody ready?" Joe glanced in the rearview mirror. He kept the sideview mirrors trained on traffic and used the rearview to keep track of the kids.

In the backseat, Linda, ten, was buckling Con,

three, into her car carrier. Linda sat up straight. "Ready." Even Linda, normally the token grump, looked bright and expectant.

Joe backed the van out into the street and they were on their way. To buy a dog.

Fel mumbled, "I can't believe we agreed to this."

"We've done some stupid things as parents, haven't we?" Joe headed south, zigging and zagging through Tempe's residential back streets, down toward Baseline.

"And this is one of the stupidest."

Now *there* was a car! Almost a full block behind, a powder-blue Jaguar was coming the same way they were. Classic car. Gorgeous.

"I saw Jennifer Fugate yesterday." Fel had relaxed a bit, probably resigning herself to the inevitable. She was good at coming to terms with life's little uglies. She was good at everything she did—at looking good, at nursing, at single-mothering. "She's really impressed that you remembered her. She asked me if you were remarried, and I said you had a wannabe on the line."

"Cute." Marie? A wannabe? Joe smiled in spite of himself. "A little premature, but cute."

"She says there's an opening coming up in the ER at Mays, and I might apply. I'd love to work with Lee, even if that Hausmann is a horse's backside."

Joe hit the light right and turned left onto Baseline without slowing. "He sure doesn't show me much, but I guess he's pretty good. I thought you wanted to finish your master's and get into nursing administration. You're not going to have time to do it working emergency."

"Money's good."

Joe shifted lanes a block ahead of the animal shelter. As he flicked his turn signal, the kids were babbling, and by the time he pulled into the lot and parked, they were vibrating up and down. They tumbled out of the van, and Linda, their spokesperson, led them inside.

Fel made no move to get out, so Joe sat too.

She studied his face. "What about Marie? You think this is the one?"

Joe shrugged. "Is it infatuation or is it love? Who knows? I'm infatuated for certain."

His sister stared at nothing out the windshield a few moments. "I'm afraid. I watch how she looks at you, and you look at her, and I'm afraid it's love. I like our arrangement, Joe. The big house in Tempe for the kids, and Tia Edna right close by to baby-sit, and your apartment in Phoenix. I like the way we swap places and I can hide in the apartment away from the kids now and then. I like the way the kids have each other, the sense of family it provides. They fit together so well for age and everything. I like the way you can provide a father figure for my three. They need a positive male so much, with their father like he is. And if you get married, that will all change."

"For crying out loud, Fel! I've known Marie less than two months and you've got me married off already."

"I don't care. I'm scared." Fel turned to look at him. "Are you still going to Wisconsin in August?"

"I have to use or lose my annual leave by September, and she has off in August. Yeah, I think so. Fel, Marie and I have been together a total of two weeks. We don't really know each other. Maybe we won't get along. You're worrying about something that might never happen."

"I'm worrying about something that probably will."

Rico called from the door. "We found one, Pop!"

Show time. Now they were going to have to act a little enthusiastic. Fel twisted and slid out her door, and Joe climbed out his.

Rico hovered by the driver-side door. "Wow! Now there's a car!"

That powder-blue Jaguar had just parked right beside them, and a redhead was getting out.

Joe felt his mouth drop open. He gathered his jaw and his wits back together as Bernice grinned and waved.

"Why, look who's here!" She came strutting over.

"Bernice Thompson, my son, Rico, and my sister, Felicidad." *Why in blazes would you show up here?* Joe burned to ask her, but he didn't.

Bernice was grinning fiendishly, fetchingly. "Dad's away a lot with business trips, so Mom and I are talking about getting a dog. You know, for protection. I thought I'd look here. I understand they hold animals sixty days, so they have a big selection."

Joe was going to speak, but Fel launched into a better explanation of the shelter's policies than Joe could have. Besides, Rico was already dragging him inside. He let the kids haul him past the smugly smiling receptionist into fluorescent-lit corridors lined with cages. Dozens of dogs were awaiting a home here. And in smaller cages suspended from the ceiling were the cats and kittens.

But he couldn't concentrate on the dogs. Bernice had followed him here—he was certain of it. But how could she know about the Tempe address? All his mail came to his Phoenix apartment. His personnel files said Phoenix. The phone book was Phoenix. This Tempe address was under Sanchez, Fel's married name. No way Bernice could know about the Sanchez connection.

Naw. He was paranoid, or flattering himself. She was ten years younger than he. She wasn't chasing him. One chance in a million they'd be in the same place at the same time, and this was it.

Joe did not believe in one-millionth chances.

"This one!" Rico and Glo were pointing out a mutt of mixed ancestry, a shaggy white dog that looked like a collie mismated to a spaniel. The dog pressed its pointy nose through the chainlink and licked Glo furiously.

"Why that one?"

"Sheesh! Just look at him, Pop! Isn't he great?"

The attendant, a girl in a ponytail and big rubber boots, stepped in beside Joe. With a smile she corrected them. "Isn't *she* great."

"It's a mutt," Linda whined. "How about this one?" She was pointing to a small boxer.

"He looks purebred." Joe looked at the attendant.

She wagged her head sadly. "It's amazing how many excellent, well-bred dogs we get in here. Pure blood. Show quality, some of them. That boxer is young. He'll grow for another few months yet. Very nice dog. It's too bad we don't have his papers."

"This one's cute too." Glo had gravitated to the next cage, where a spaniel sort with an equally long tongue went into its adopt-me act.

"You know, Pop," Rico mused, "I'd take anything here. They're all good. You should be the one to pick one out, because you don't like dogs as much as we do. Pick one that *you* like best."

"It's not going to be my dog."

"But you gotta live with it."

"He's not picking *my* dog out," Linda huffed.

Joe walked over to Linda and gave her a side-by-side hug. "We'll make sure everyone's happy with the choice, Lin."

"Choices." Fel drew Joe aside. "Plural. I've decided we're getting two."

"Fel . . . !"

"One for your kids and one for mine. That way, when we break up into separate families, we won't have a big custody battle over the dog."

"You're so sure I'm getting married."

"Or me. Who knows? Maybe my Charlie will get struck by lightning and realize he wants to be a family man. You know and I know this arrangement isn't going to last forever. You and Glo and Rico pick out whatever you want. And we'll choose ours."

Joe studied her a moment. She was slim and pretty, a nurse at the top of her profession, intelligent and kind. It was a miracle she wasn't remarried already. She was right. Fel was usually right about practical stuff. He grimaced and nodded.

Rico and Glo had already chosen two others as

the best and were working on the cage at the end. Joe squatted down and instantly Glo plopped onto the seat his leg made for her. She wrapped one thin little arm around his neck and with the other pointed to just about every dog in the cage.

At almost ten, Rico considered himself too old to snuggle, so he just sidled up to Joe and pressed close. "You know, Pop? That real big mutt near the back, lying down. See him?"

"Black and shaggy."

"Yeah! He's been watching every move we make. See how his ears are up? But he's too macho to beg. He won't—" Rico waved a hand, trying to find his word in thin air.

"Won't lower himself?"

"Yeah. Exactly. He's dignified. How about him, Glo? You said you wanted a big happy dog."

"Will he jump all around? I don't want a dog that jumps all around. They're scary."

Joe gave her a squeeze. "We'll make sure he's a quiet sort before we take him."

Quick as a bunny, the attendant stepped up to the cage door. She pointed to the big dog. "You. Come on, boy." She gestured *come*.

The mutt lurched to his feet and came ambling over. He walked out the door casually, with aplomb. The dog stood nearly St. Bernard size and had to weigh close to 200 pounds. His jowls hung, making his face look charmingly woebegone. But he obviously wasn't young. He didn't have that puppy bounce. Joe had heard that older dogs require less food.

Glo wrapped her arms around his neck and the

most wonderful smile spread across her face. "He's soft. He's so soft, Pop!"

"He's probably pure Newfoundland," the attendant commented. "Newfs are silky soft. And he's one of our best behaved."

Rico was grinning too. "He's perfect!"

"Both kids agreeing on something." Joe dropped down on one knee to get a better look at the dog. He had read you should look for clear, bright, attentive eyes. Check. And clean ears and teeth. Check. And a glossy, healthy looking coat. Check.

He nodded to the attendant. "We'd better take him quick before they see something else."

All achatter with glee, Glo wrapped around Joe's neck in a spontaneous hug. Even Rico hugged him briefly. "Thanks, Pop! This is great! Thanks!"

And then Joe noticed Bernice. She stood down by the first cages cuddling a puppy, but the puppy could have been chewing her arm off for all the attention she paid it. She was staring at Joe, at Joe and his kids.

She was trying to smile, to no avail. Unceremoniously she dumped the puppy out of her arms onto the walkway. As she wheeled to run out, her face was clouding up into tears. Joe heard the front door slam.

Moments later he heard the Jaguar roar away.

Dry-Eyed Mourner

No one was investigating robberies in Phoenix today. The whole division, from Pete Marks to the file clerks, crowded into the little stucco church on Seventh Avenue. Mighty Mouse's parents sat in the front row along with two brothers and a sister. Joe had never met them before. The pews were full, the walls lined two and three deep. An inspecting fire marshall would have suffered a coronary. Why did they choose this small church for the funeral? Probably because it was Mouse's.

An 11 x 14 glossy of Mouse sat on the closed casket. There were flowers, but not mountains of them. Joe remembered the request at the bottom of the newspaper obituary – please make a contribution to a worthy charity in lieu of flowers.

Gretchen squirmed, pressed by the crush of people

against Joe's left arm. "I mastered my tendency to cry at weddings; I figure if she wants to be that stupid, the bride doesn't deserve tears. But funerals still get me. Be prepared."

"Forewarned is forearmed." From his coat pocket Tom fished a wad of folded nose tissue big enough to choke a shark.

"You beautiful man!" Gretchen grinned. "I don't think I brought near enough."

The usual organ prelude and the invocation set Joe on edge instantly. He hated funerals. He thought about Louise's funeral, and the hired preacher's sappy words. His wife, Louise, died in the act of running off with her lover. Cuckolding Joe, leaving their kids alone in the house, and Glo still in diapers. Yet, by the time the preacher finished his eulogy, she was the madonna of Maricopa County. Maybe even all Arizona.

If he hadn't been so numb with grief and pain, Joe would have kicked the pastor in the behind and corrected the sermon right there. He still felt like doing it, nearly five years later.

Mouse's pastor stepped to the lectern. He was much younger than Joe. He smiled. Smiled? At a funeral?

"Friends, we're here to honor the memory of Marsha Laine, better known as Mouse, and to celebrate her graduation—graduation from mortality to immortality. Her gravestone will record her body's age as twenty-three years, five months, and nine days. Her soul graduated at age seven months, almost to the day. You see, seven months ago is when she was born into the family of God by committing her life to Jesus Christ."

A bolt of relief mixed with a twinge of conscience, robbing Joe's attention. The relief: Mouse was in heaven now, despite that he had not mentioned anything about Jesus to her as she lay dying. He was astonished at the load he felt lifting off his heart.

The conscience: He had made an identical commitment to Jesus Christ in the presence of Marie Kabrhan two months ago. She had drawn it from him in a moment of extremity, but that did not dismiss the fact that he had promised to honor it, to stick with it. At the time, that commitment had seemed so right. He could feel the difference in him; he knew that conversion is real. When he read the Bible now, it meant infinitely more to him. But since then he had not been consistently reading the Bible she gave him. Neither was he consistent in worship or prayer or any other thing. He was drifting. Maybe this Sunday he'd bring the kids here. It seemed like a good church, a place Marie would like, a place to grow in.

Marie. He'd call her this evening. Again. She was still in Waukesha, preparing to come to Phoenix job-seeking in the autumn. His phone bill looked like the price tag on a solid gold sports car.

". . . fall away. But Mouse did not . . ."

Fall away. His conscience prickled again.

". . . grew tremendously, even in those seven short months." The preacher paused and chuckled. He leaned forward on his lectern, abandoning his notes. "I remember this one prayer meeting. Mouse was sitting right about there." He pointed. "We were talking about how Jesus alters the life devoted to Him, when a young man stood up. I don't know what he was popping, but he was high. Abusive. He started contradicting, spraying expletives in everyone's ears. And Mouse sat right beside him."

Someone in the pews murmured. The preacher continued. "He was getting more disruptive than I could handle—wouldn't listen to reason, of course. So Mouse stood up beside him. The top of her head stopped just short of his armpit. She suggested he step outside and she'd explain the Gospel for him. He yelled at her. All of a sudden she moved, not much, mind you, and he was upside down. I mean, there his blue and green shoes were flying through the air. One each—one blue, one green."

Several laughed. The pastor swung an arm in the air. "She must've tossed him this high! She put a hammerlock on him and said, 'Now listen!' and y'know, he listened. He had no choice."

Joe found himself grinning. Yes, that was Mouse.

"So you see, her conversion to the faith in no way changed her personally. It redirected her. I hear people complain that Christianity is wishy-washy. Mouse would be the first to tell you it's no such thing. I wish. . . ."

A young man near the wall stood up suddenly. "I'm the guy you're talking about. It was me. What little Mouse did to me, y'know, that was an act of love. It was an act of love 'cause I wouldn't listen to the Gospel any other way. Because of her, I found a reason to live. I get flashes now and then yet, but I'm off the stuff. All of it. I praise the Lord He sent me Mouse that night."

A girl down in the second row stood up. "You don't have to be looking for better living through chemistry to be all messed up. I had it made—a wealthy boyfriend, nice apartment, good job in traffic control. Mouse showed me none of that was giving me any satisfaction. I was still empty on the inside. She showed me how Jesus satisfies. This is the first time in my life I'm really, truly happy, since Mouse brought me to Jesus."

Three rows behind her an office clerk stood up sobbing. "I thought Mouse was putting me on, and I was mad at her for trying to stuff her religion down my throat. Now I see she was doing it because she cared about me." She shuddered. "It's not too late, is it, Mouse?"

The pastor stepped down off his dais. "Not at all." He smiled at the girl. "Come. Let me show you what Mouse sees." He hopped the railing, wrapped an arm around the young woman, and drew her aside right there.

Joe caught himself gaping. Of all places to. . . .

Maude Drummond, the jail matron, stood up. "Mouse had her ways, all right. I remember this one night she was on cell block duty after supper. Wait. Maybe I better explain to you folks who don't know what the inside of women's detention is like. The women are kept in cell blocks linked by corridors to the dining room. The different cell blocks take turns on kitchen duty—help out the cooks, wipe the tables.

"Well, this one night, Mouse's block had kitchen duty. Her women had just left the dining area and were coming back when Blanche phoned her. 'Thirty ice-cream bars are missing out of the freezer,' Blanche says, 'and your girls probably took them.' So here come Mouse's inmates down the corridor and she sees them coming through the one-way glass. 'Wait there a minute, girls,' she says ever so sweetly. And she lets them just stand there. And stand there.

"Now you see, jail clothes don't have pockets. There's only one place to hide an ice-cream bar. No, two. When Mouse finally let her girls back into their block, you shoulda seen 'em. Melted ice cream and chocolate was running down their legs, oozing out of embarrassing places."

The floodgates opened, with laughter. One after another, anxious and orderly, Mouse's friends told stories on her—good-humored stories warmly remembered. When the pastor returned to his lectern, even her parents were laughing.

As people turned to look at first this speaker and then that one, Joe could see profiles and sometimes full faces. Who was not here who ought to be? Who was here who ought not to be? He saw no mourners out of the ordinary in this sea of faces to the front and sides.

"What can I say?" The preacher raised his hands helplessly. "You have just praised Mouse more eloquently than any eulogy of mine ever could. I can't add to her stature by sermonizing. I don't have to. But I want to give every one of you here the message that was at the forefront of her daily walk—the message she pressed upon anyone who would listen. Only through Jesus do you gain true life, and then you can do those works that will live with you into eternity. Those of you who want to share Mouse's joy and purpose, I invite you to come forward right here. Come and accept God's free gift of Jesus, as Mouse did. Then come walk with Mouse's body and me to her body's final resting place."

"Mother MacCrea!" Tom muttered. "An altar call at a funeral. Amazing!" His wad of tissue, now gripped in Gretchen's fist, was a fourth its original size.

People surged forward, a score of them. More. Gretchen twisted beside Joe. She was sobbing violently, her purse stuffed with spent tissue. She stood up and forced her way past Joe to join the newly committed pouring down the aisle.

Joe turned to survey the faces behind him. In a pale-blue sundress, she blended in well with the genuine mourners. She stood by the huge, carved double doors, poised to fly. Bernice.

Joe poked Tom, mumbled in his ear, and started up the aisle. Bernice saw him instantly and disappeared out the doors.

Joe bolted out the side door and jogged across the parking lot. She was marching, with strides as long as three-inch heels would allow, across the lot toward her classic powder-blue Jaguar. He reached the car a second ahead of her and leaned against the door on the driver's side. She stopped a moment, then stepped forward boldly. She planted herself right in front of him, as brassy as ever.

He smiled. "To what do we owe the pleasure of your attendance?"

"I always wondered what the funeral of a role model was like. Different. I'll say that for it. My grandmother would turn over in her coffin if she got one like this."

"If you happen to get one like this, what will all your friends and relations have to say about you?"

"I couldn't care less because I won't be around to listen to them. Unless you're going to make a pass—at a funeral, yet—get away from my car." Her lovely eyes were dry and clear.

"Will you be attending Lawrence Banks' funeral too?"

"I wouldn't tell you if your fly was open, Hiawatha."

His eyes dropped involuntarily.

". . . even if it was true. Gotcha!" She shouldered him aside and slipped into her driver's seat. She jammed the key into the ignition. The Jag roared. "Don't take any wooden Indian-head nickels." She put a hand on the gearshift and paused. "So what if I paid respects to the deceased?"

"We frequently take movies of everyone at a murder victim's funeral, because it's a known fact that the killer often attends. Casts an interesting light on your presence here."

A fleeting look of bemusement—but not fear—softened her face. "Marvelous, Geronimo! Keep guessing." She popped it into reverse, bolted backward, and peeled away. A faint smell of burnt rubber and a strong smell of exhaust were all Bernice left behind.

Petroglyph Hunters

Joe leaned back against the No Parking sign in front of police headquarters as he unbuttoned his cuffs and rolled the sleeves barely to his elbows. He yawned. He was going to have to give up these nights of wild carousing if he was going to get up this early. Carousing. He half smiled. He glanced at his watch. Tom had better give up carousing too; he was late.

A familiar blue Jaguar hummed by, the only vehicle on the street. It screeched to a halt, roared into reverse and came backing up to park at the red curb in front of Joe's blue Chevy Suburban.

Bernice popped up and stood on her seat to lean back against the windshield bar. She wore a skimpy white tennis outfit. "I bet you were waiting for some cute little chick to drive by and say hello."

"I still am." Joe reached up and rapped the No

Parking sign with his knuckles.

"Monkey see, monkey do." She pointed to his illegally parked Suburban. "Nice comeback. I was afraid for a while you were too straight to do well at cut-cut. What'd you do yesterday after the funeral? After your Mouse was all properly tucked away?"

"Took."

"Took what?"

"Took Gretchen over to Calvary Bookstore to buy her the Bible of her choice. Took Tom down to the VW dealership to get points and plugs for his Bug. Took my laundry over to my sister's. Took the kids out for supper at the Extraburger, all of them. Then took them to see that sci-fi flick at Chris-Town. Took them home. Took a shower, went to bed. You asked."

"All the kids? Those kids at the shelter?"

Joe nodded.

She wrinkled her nose. "You voluntarily took a three-year-old to the movies? That's masochism!"

"My sister needs time alone now and then. Besides, Con's a sweet little kid. Bright. Upbeat." He paused. "Respectful."

"That's your big theme, isn't it . . . respect. And I think you used 'cherish' once. I'm supposed to cherish all this wonderful life I lead. Your preaching is getting a little thin."

"I know too many people who don't have the things you're spitting on—family, comfort, home. If you don't like the lectures, don't burn rubber parking at a red curb."

"Con. What's Con short for?"

"Consuelo. My sister's ex-husband hates the

name, but she likes it."

"Vindictive witch, your sister."

"That's what her ex says. She's just bitter because Con was conceived six months after their estrangement, when he came by drunk one night and forced her."

"Charming family relationships, all of you. How's the new dog doing?"

"Dogs. Two dogs. Fel's kids picked out a cocker spaniel. The spaniel's doing fine, but we haven't quite convinced the Newf that I'm a member of the family."

She grinned. "What's that mean? The dog bite you?"

"He was thinking about it for a while there, defending his turf. He'll be a first-class watchdog."

"Here comes your partner. Bet you're going on a picnic."

"Bet you're playing tennis. When's your date?"

"Twenty minutes ago. He can wait."

Tom bobbed to a halt beside Joe and hefted a styro cooler. "Top o' the mornin' to ye, Miss Thompson!" He turned to Joe. "Bought a takeout at Chicken King last night and refrigerated it. Should keep just fine till lunch. Six-pack of cola, six-pack of lemon-lime. That should do it, ye think?"

"Sounds fine." Joe raised his voice and flapped a mitt at the Jaguar. "Sorry to run out on you like this, Miss Thompson." He ambled around to climb in behind the steering wheel.

Tom humped the cooler and his bag of goodies into the back and crawled up into the passenger side. "Don't let a cop see ye parked at that red curb,

Miss Thompson. Toodle-oo." He took his wide-brimmed hat off and tossed it into the seat behind. He lowered his voice as Joe started the engine. "Toodle-oo, indeed. How'd she happen on our doorstep at this ungodly hour?"

Joe pulled out into Washington Street and gave it a little extra kick to make the corner light in time. "I've been calculating that. I doubt she'd stoop to using public courts. There aren't any country clubs down here, so she swung a couple miles out of her way just to cruise the station."

"Sounds like quite a crush she has on ye." Tom giggled. He didn't chuckle; he giggled.

"Probably just seeking opportunities to needle me. She enjoys being as nasty as possible to me."

"A fine line of distinction, easily blurred." Tom settled deeper in the bucket seat. "Have ye met this Schumacher ever?"

"Never even talked to her on the phone."

"Sounds x-rated, this expedition of hers, Vale Schumacher and Brent Sommers out seeking rocks together. Out alone on the desert with a macho young man, ostensibly hunting petroglyphs. A setup if ever I saw one. Simplifies our task, though. Interview two birds we want to talk to, and with one stone—one petroglyph, if ye will."

"I think it's legit. Purley got the same feeling. Brent Sommers has more than a passing interest in native art and Schumacher's an expert in it. Sommers is out surveying petroglyphs with his wife's blessing, according to the Burl. Mrs. Sommers trusts them, and she doesn't want to fry in the summer sun for the sake of looking at ancient graffiti. Not even Otis Burnside seems to see anything amiss."

"Then this Schumacher can't be much to look at." Tom shifted, fidgety, and they weren't yet out of town. He did not ride well in this high, boxy four-by. Probably because of his little green beetle, he was more a small-car man. "Burnside. Ye remarked on his wedding ring. He not only knows where all the silver is, he knows all the silversmiths, by virtue of running the craft festivals. He must have considerable skill in planning too."

"You think he's planning burglary as well?"

"Perfect situation. All he need do is accidentally lose his key ring, or duplicate the relevant keys. He sets the burglar up, then knows best where to dispose of the loot afterward. Carefully maintains his own appearance of innocence, of course."

"So what's his connection to Lawrence Banks? Or Mouse?"

"A tenuous possibility—Banks is Bernice's boyfriend. Burnside has been a guest more'n once at Thompsons. He might well have met Lawrence there, just as he apparently met this George the gardener."

"Only hitch—why would Bernice take up with a convicted felon like Banks in the first place?"

"To spite her mother."

"I'll buy that."

Tom settled into silent thought, and Joe did too. He thought about Marie in Waukesha, and about how fast his kids were growing. He thought about how well his sister was coping. And he thought about Bernice. He glanced in the rearview mirror frequently, half expecting to see a powder-blue Jag back there, but apparently Bernice was playing tennis now.

South of Chandler Joe left the freeway, drove two miles down a feeder road and bumped off onto a dirt track.

"Be ye certain ye know where we're going?"

"Schumacher's secretary said northwest of Bapchule somewhere. The only petroglyphs I know of should be somewhere within 500 square miles of us right now. Tan Land Rover with international orange roof. Now you know as much as I do."

"Not at all heartening. Here we be in the midst of a midsummer inferno and as lost as a flea on a buffalo."

Despite that Joe had specified the optional back vents, the air conditioning in the Suburban didn't come near cooling the interior. The best it could do if the temp topped 100 was move the air around a little. Presently Tom stripped his shirt off and sat sweating in partial dishabille, a woefully misplaced Irishman in the broiling desert.

They couldn't go fast enough to leave the dust behind. It boiled up and around—gritty and penetrating. The only words spoken for nearly an hour were Tom's, "This casts quite a pall upon your wax job, Jose."

Joe's grandfather had brought his father and himself this way many times to see the petroglyphs. But the freeway didn't pass by then, nor did roads go the same places they seemed to be going now. Joe negotiated the ungraded track with considerable care; his 'Burb lurched crazily over rocks and ruts. This particular track, though, had been used frequently in the recent past. Its dirt was stirred, its stones loose.

Short scraggly bushes gave way to larger solitary bushes and occasional saguaros as they gained elevation. The road twisted and bucked and squeezed between low outcrops. They topped out on a gentle hill.

Tom sat up straighter. "Now what's that?"

"Looks like an international orange roof."

"Jose, me lad, you're a genius! A marvel of navigational expertise. Brilliant maneuvering across the boundless waste."

"Hold your praise; I haven't gotten us back out yet."

"You're putting me on, I hope."

The 'Burb jolted down across the hillside. Joe parked beside the Land Rover and climbed out, happy indeed to get his hands off the vibrating steering wheel at last. He made mental note to realign the front end soon and check the universal joints and suspension.

Tommy stayed behind him as he walked a wide circle around the Rover, reading the ground. He pointed soundlessly to the traces he saw, more a tutorial for Tommy than an explanation. Tommy was getting pretty good at tracking too.

Two people had left the vehicle on foot, angling into the rocks to the northwest. The larger of the two pairs of vibram-soled boots followed behind the smaller. Both the vehicle and the hikers had been here at least twice before in the last few days.

"Too many hours till lunch and not a soul

around." Tom uncapped the gallon canteen. "So how shall we while away the time?" He drank and passed the jug to Joe. The water was warm.

"They're probably in shouting distance, up among those rocks there. You're turning into a lobster. Want to hang around the car? I'll go see if they're close." Joe gave the canteen back and pulled a pair of binoculars out of the van's jump box.

Distant stones rattled high among the rocks beyond the Rover. A dissheveled brown head appeared on the skyline. Joe swung the binoculars up and fiddled with the seesaw focus. The young man was no outdoorsman. He picked his way down with difficulty, lurching and stumbling. Twenty feet down the hill he paused to glance toward the Rover. He froze and stared at Joe watching him through the glasses. His face rearranged itself by degrees into composure, even say confidence. Here he came again. He stumbled toward the vehicles and leaned against the Land Rover.

Joe held out his badge at an angle conducive to easy viewing. "Joe Rodriguez. My partner, Tom Flaherty. We're looking for Vale Schumacher. You must be Brent Sommers."

"I am. How do you do?" He pocketed a ring of keys and reached for a handshake.

Tom accepted. "Me pleasure."

"Dr. Schumacher's still up there. I'll bring her down for you." He turned away without bothering to shake Joe's hand.

"Eh, no reason to trouble yourself. Ye look near spent already. Just point the general direction and we'll look her up. No need to interrupt your digging, or whatever it is ye anthropologists do."

The art museum director smiled coldly. "No, I insist. I'll go get her. I know just where she is. Wait here."

Tom must have detected the same false note Joe heard, for he moved in close on the man's other side. "No, 'tis we who insist, lad. We go along."

Brent Sommers looked from face to face. "What is this, anyway? Why did you two come clear out here?"

"To talk to you both. Besides, it's a nice day for a picnic. May I see the keys?" Joe held out his hand.

Sommers eyed him suspiciously and fished out the ring. In addition to keys it carried a C-ration can opener and one of those "drop in any mailbox" tags with Schumacher's name and the Heldt Museum address.

Sommers waved a hand carelessly. "Those are Dr. Schumacher's keys. She sent me back here for some things. Gave me her keys."

"But the Rover's unlocked and all its windows are open." Joe usurped the ring.

"Guess we forgot. The heat, you know."

A distant movement caught Joe's eye. High up in the rocks, a lean figure in faded jeans moved among the boulders and scrub.

"Don't go away." Joe handed the binoculars to Tom and jogged off across the stove-hot caliche. He felt lightheaded, hurrying so in this heat. The woman sat down on a rock and watched him. He slowed to a walk and started the climb toward her, picking his way boulder to boulder. Did the ghosts and monsters guarding Yaqui silver bother themselves with petroglyphs? Did they prowl abroad in day, as these mad dogs and Englishmen were doing, or did they wait until the dark of the moon for their mischief?

He tried to approach her in a somewhat dignified manner, but dignity doesn't dance well with rock-hopping.

"Dr. Schumacher?"

"I am." A fresh scuff across her left cheek oozed a few little beads of dark blood.

"Joe Rodriguez, Phoenix homicide. Can I help you?"

Even soggy with perspiration, she seemed somehow starched and superefficient. "Thank you, I'm all right. Just resting a moment. I learned long ago never to overexert at this time of year. You did say homicide?" Her hair flew free in a sort of Amelia Earhart style. There were a few streaks of gray in it, but all in all she looked remarkably young and spry for a woman in her mid-fifties.

Joe sat down on a rock near her. "Tom and I came out to ask you a few questions—you and Mr. Sommers. We were told you'd be out here three or four days yet, and we didn't want to wait that long for answers. Besides, an outing even this time of year is better than beating the pavement in town." He shifted to face her more squarely. "Did we just break in on something unpleasant?"

Her voice stayed cucumber crisp. "Unpleasant is a relative term. Many would say this heat is unpleasant. I don't mind it. We came to catalog a series of petroglyphs before vandals discover them—rubbings, photos, mapping, and so forth. That's precisely what we're doing; call it unpleasant if you will."

"You're misreading me deliberately. Mr. Sommers was interested in more than petroglyphs; am I right?"

"It's unseemly to disguise innuendo as insight."

"I was watching his face as he came off the hill; the face of a man intent on driving away in a fit of pique and leaving you stranded."

"You've a remarkable flair for drama, Mr. . . . ah, Rodriguez, is it? Is this what you traveled all the way out here to ask?" Her face under the best of circumstances was gaunt, and the stress of the summer heat made it a death mask. Her frame was devoid of any spare ounce or rounded curve. She was one of those people who reaches age forty-five in her twentieth year and stays there for fifty years longer. She held his eye comfortably. She could have stared down a marble statue.

Joe sighed and settled forward, his elbows on his knees. He should have drunk more of Tom's warm water. In the distance below Tom was leaning on the Rover as he engaged Sommers in earnest conversation. "You left town before all this happened—just before, in fact. We received a tip that a major theft of silver is imminent. We notified your Mr. Burnside as well as other prime targets."

"What has this to do with homicide?"

"The tipster and a policewoman have been murdered, apparently in connection with the possible theft." Joe shifted. Heat from the rock was penetrating his clothing. How could she sit there so serenely? "Mr. Burnside is more or less in charge of silver—is that correct?"

"Yes. It's his interest and he's the best. Mine is baskets, shards, and petroglyphs."

"Has he been making any unusual additions, deletions, or changes in either the vault or the display collection?"

"Why do you ask?"

Joe looked at her. "Because it's relevant to the case." He did not add that this particular topic seemed to make Burnside very uncomfortable.

She nodded. "I'm sure the fact that I see no relevance doesn't mean there is none. He's always shifting pieces, especially as we acquire new items. I don't concern myself with details of that sort. That's his area."

"Mr. Sommers represents the art museum. This is a joint expedition, so to speak? Do Heldt and Phoenix Art ever exchange pieces? Not just silver—any objects?"

"We used to loan material to each other for special exhibits. We don't bother anymore; too much hassle. Our collections are housed within a few blocks of each other. Hardly any point to it."

"The display in the art museum now is from out of town. Does Heldt ever contribute pieces to traveling exhibits of that sort?"

"Now and then, for large, significant tours, or shows of one particular artist's work. We've provided the display for the big glass case in the new Sky Harbor Building, the fourth annex there. We'll be bringing that back soon, though. They're changing the exhibit."

"I stop at that case every time I'm in the airport.

That big Pima basket, especially, is a beauty. Think a moment. Have you any observations that might help us—suspicious circumstances recently, furtive employees, unusual or repetitive visitors—anything of that sort?"

She took in air and studied the distant Land Rover awhile. "No. Phoenix seems to be getting more than its share of strange people these last few years. Perhaps the climate draws them. And an assortment of rather strange types prowls our museum. But none that I remember would suggest a person capable of dropping two people in their tracks. We do have a lot of repetitive visits, but they're mostly retired people."

"Any unusual problems with security? False alarms? System failures?"

"No. Mr. Burnside and Mr. Cleaver take care of that." She stood up. "Shall we continue?"

"Certainly. Tommy and I just happened to bring lunch for four, hoping you might join us." He stayed close by her side as they threaded down through the rocks. "Any major arguments with Mr. Burnside lately?"

"He never argues. But no, no disagreements."

"You trust him completely?"

"Surely that's obvious. I'm out here and he's minding the store."

"Mr. Sommers—you trust him?"

"No farther than I can throw him."

"Which is what you tried to do a few minutes ago and lost."

"That's the second or third approach you've made. You're being too obvious. Cavorting about in these rocks is risky for the nimblest of youngsters, and I'm neither nimble nor young. I scuffed my face falling. Period. Embarrassing, but an occupational hazard."

"Your occupation is museum director. Why are you out here in the middle of nowhere under the summer sun?"

"I'm a recognized expert in ethnology who made my reputation with good fieldwork. I love fieldwork. From October through Easter I'm much too busy to lavish time gallivanting in the field. Summer's my only slack. Ergo, I'm out in the middle of nowhere in the summer sun."

"Why bring Mr. Sommers? Why not another ethnologist or anthropologist?"

"He's interested in ethnic art and there's no way to see these petroglyphs except to come out here and look at them. He asked me to bring him along, so I did. It's not a joint expedition as such."

They were approaching the vehicles. Tom and Sommers were rummaging around in back of the Rover.

"You know Lawrence Banks, Dr. Schumacher?"

She paused and stood thinking a moment. "No. I can't place the name." Her face handled it just right—the confusion seemed genuine. "Is he associated with Heldt?"

"Not that we know of. The information could be spurious."

"Check our membership roster and mailing list, but I don't recall the name." She started forward again.

Tom and Sommers were erecting some sort of

portable awning, a shade frame. Joe returned the doctor's keys to her and broke out the chicken and six-packs. The lady was being evasive, but Joe had no idea how or where. What she said sounded genuine, but what she did not say nagged at the edges of his thoughts. He didn't know how to pry it loose.

Lunch came and went. Although the two were not together constantly this past week—frequently they separated for one reason or another—their joint alibi rang true. Joe got a solid feeling, later corroborated by Tom, that Schumacher cared very little for this young man fate dumped in her lap, and that she avoided his company whenever possible.

Schumacher and Sommers, heads together, assayed what they had accomplished, declared it to be enough, and decided to return early to civilization. Both seemed concerned that Pete Marks' tip might be true. They caravaned out soon after lunch, the Rover and the Suburban, and Joe felt smug in the fact that his high and waddling secondhand rig could keep pace with the costly Rover they were following. It took them less than two hours to reach the stoplights of downtown Phoenix.

But that nagging feeling that something was missing, that something important remained unsaid, would not go away.

Cardoon Wrestler

If the Phoenix zoo was Joe's favorite and most familiar place to visit, the Desert Botanical Garden came a close second. It sprawled down across a small drainage in a nether corner of Papago Park, an inconspicuous and sun-drenched repository of cactus and other desert plants, a vegetable zoo displaying the flora of Joe's Indian and Mexican heritage. He brought the kids here once a year, usually at the height of the spring bloom. Every year he stopped by the Garden's fund-raising plant sale to buy something for his sister's cactus garden. Frequently, though, he would visit alone at odd hours and off season, to wander among the plantings. He knew everything here by name and habitat.

He waited his turn now at the inside desk as Tom wandered from one display counter to another. The

Garden's gift shop might be small, but they carried some nice items. A lady in a florid muumuu eyed her newly purchased box of cactus. "I plant these with lots of little stones on the bottom, right?"

Elderly Mr. Bergman was volunteering in the gift shop today. "Yes, madam. The instructions in the box are very clear."

"But I don't live here. I live in Michigan. How will I know when to water them?"

"Follow the printed instructions, madam."

"But these are Arizona instructions. My cactus will be in my house, in Michigan. How much do I water them there?"

Mr. Bergman displayed only a trace of exasperation. "I suggest, if you don't trust the printed instructions, that you subscribe to the Phoenix paper. When the paper says it rained, water them."

Blessed are the peacemakers. Joe stepped up smiling and assumed his Spanish accent. "Eh'scuse me, señora. My sister, she keeps cactus inna house. She waters it two times a month, 'cept not in August or September. Don' water at all, then."

"Thank you." The woman scowled at Mr. Bergman and walked away to look at the Hong Kong "silver" earrings.

Mr. Bergman wagged his gray head. "And how are you today, Mr. Rodriguez?"

Joe ditched the accent. "Fine. Here on business this time. Is a George Varendes in today?"

"George? Yes. Quiet old George. The police want to talk to George?"

"In this town, it's not what you do but what you know. He may know some things we need without even realizing it. He knows a lot of people, goes a lot of places."

"That he does. Try Baja. I think he's there."

"Subscribe to the paper, huh?" Joe grinned and walked out the back door into the garden. Tom fell in beside him. The place looked deserted this time of year; a few shriveled stalks marked the graves of a million spring wildflowers that would leap to life come next April, to dazzle the senses again. The barrel cactus was blooming now, but that was about all.

"And how is the new dog coming?" Tommy seemed not the least interested in anything here.

"He's territorial."

Tom snickered. "By which I surmise he bit ye."

"Not yet. Just threatened, is all. He doesn't think I live there."

"He's right, ye know. Ye just pass through on occasion."

"Yeah. And buy his dog food." Maybe Fel was right. Maybe Marie would change all that, and he and his kids could be a family again at last.

"I would suppose that be George in the distance there." Tom pointed in the general direction of the cluster of boogum trees. All Joe could see were the absurd, upside-down white carrots. A blue shirt moved into view behind them. "Eh, but how do we get there from here?"

"This way." Joe backtracked the path to a little arching bridge, crossed the wash and came up on Baja California from the far side.

George Varendes was trying to dig to China via Phoenix, and he was a good three feet on his way.

Beside him, partly blocking the walkway, lay a spiny man-sized cactus, a fatter and more bristly version of a saguaro.

Joe stepped across the giant's dusty root system, from the walkway domain of the visitor into the never-never land to be trod only by employees. George stood up straight in his hole and scowled.

Joe flashed his badge. "Jose Rodriguez, homicide. Señor Varendes?"

"Si . . ." A deeper scowl.

"Tom Flaherty. Me pleasure." Tom definitely looked the outsider, a redhead among Hispanics. "Would ye mind sitting a few minutes to answer some questions?"

"S'pose to set this cardoon, and a coupla other things. Then I gotta go to Thompsons yet today, plant some roses . . ." His voice trailed away.

Tom stared at the cactus. "Hulking bugger and then some. Anyone who can wrestle this porcupine to a standstill has me vote, for sure. Let us help ye, since we're putting ye behind."

"Uh, I don' . . ."

"Good. Now how do we manhandle this beast?"

"Jus' a minute." George picked up his shovel and subjected his hole to further excavation.

Joe felt like shouting, George seemed so distant down in that hole. "We're interested primarily in a Mr. Burnside over at the Heldt Museum. We understand you know him."

"I don't know no Burnside. Oh. The museum." George stood erect. "You mean Otis?"

"Otis Burnside. Yes."

"I know him, yeah."

"Where did you meet him? Remember?"

George hacked at his hole. "Thompsons. Yeah, Thompsons. Thass where I met him."

"The Whitney Thompsons, up on Camelback?"

He nodded impatiently.

"He go to Thompsons often?"

"I see him there once or twice."

Tom jumped into the conversation. "Meself has heard that he pays ye special attention, that the two of ye be close."

"Yeah, I guess." George averted his eyes.

Tom skated away. "Ah, that's nice. Mrs. Thompson. She must be a peach to work for."

"Always wants you do a lot. More'n you have time for. But she pays good."

"Ye must have a long list of clients ye work for. Dozens."

George climbed out of his hole. "Thompsons. Here. Kinneys. Mrs. Bevins. Otis sometimes. Rackhams. Just six." He reversed his shovel with a practiced flick and used the handle to drag the tangled root end of the cactus over the hole.

"Would ye know a young man named Lawrence Banks?"

"Whass he look like?"

"About this tall, blond, well built, bearded."

"Lawrence? Larry?"

"Aye."

George shook his head. "Ain' the same one. This Larry hung around Thompsons awhile. Boyfriend of Bernice. The daughter. But no beard. Beard is mess up his suntan."

"Do ye much gardening for Mr. Burnside?"

"He don' have much yard work. I hung those planters at the museum, though—designed them and hung them. Otis hired me for that."

"At Heldt?" Joe asked. "Those terra-cotta pots hanging in the arches around the central patio? Nice piece of work."

George tried to smile and couldn't. He straddled his hole and grabbed the giant cardoon by its roots. He yanked about, positioning it just so. "You wanna help? Haul it up there; the straps."

With serious misgivings Joe took up the ends of two heavy leather belts double-looped around the cactus and gripped them in his good left hand. Tom took the other ends and together they heaved upward. Waggling wickedly and threatening with its spikes, the cactus lurched to near upright. George directed the root end and it dropped *thunk* into its new home. How would George have managed without them?

Tom hung onto his end with one hand and popped the other in his mouth a moment. "Tell me something, George. Might I call ye George? This Mr. Burnside won't let me be so chummy. How did ye get him to let ye call him Otis? I'd love to be that close to him meself."

Joe almost smiled. As if he didn't know Tom had never actually spoken to Burnside....

"People who help each other oughta be friends, he says. We're friends."

"He sends work your way now and then? So what do ye do for him?"

George began shoveling dirt into the hole with mad exuberance. "Gardening. You know, jus' gardening. Is what I do."

Tom glanced at Joe. There was something here. George flicked that shovel into reverse again snake-quick and used the handle to tamp dirt around the roots. Another flick and he was shoveling more dirt into the hole.

Tom cooed, "Must be heaven for a gardener like yourself to work here. These magnificent specimens from deserts all over the world. Your own skill in caring for 'em . . . can't be easy. 'Tis like Mr. Burnside and his museum full of silver—best in the world. Here ye are with a garden full of cactus, the best in the world."

"Lahssa people have silver. Nobody got plants like these."

"True, true." Tom snapped his fingers. "Ah, but that Mrs. Thompson has some spendid saguaros in her yard. I saw 'em."

"I planted them. I put them saguaros in for her."

"There, ye see, Joe? As I was telling ye, that Mrs. Thompson has the best of everything—fine saguaros, splendid garden, and that Royce Howard silver as well."

"Otis, he says is too good for just one rich bitch. Says it oughta be in a museum, that silver, let the whole world see it, y'know?" George stopped cold and licked his lips. He began tamping furiously.

"He said that, eh? How about Miss Thompson—the daughter? She ever talk about the silver in her house much?"

"She don' say nothing 'bout nothing, less it's complaining. Stuck-up. The two boys, they was never stuck-up. The boys both died. But she is. Hey.

Got other stuff. I gotta go."

"Mmmm. Then, George, we best not keep ye from your appointed rounds here. Enjoyed immensely talking with ye." Tom extended his hand and George obliged.

Joe shook two-handed, and added a few words of grace and parting in Spanish. George's hands were calloused to the hardness of rawhide. He worked hard, did George Varendes.

Tom looked a bit confused, so Joe led the way, up the path past the fairyduster *(Calliandra eryophylla)* and desertwillow *(Chilopsis linearis)*, along the winding walk toward the main entrance.

"Methinks, Joe, that Burnside has more in this than we've been giving him credit for."

"Pete's division or ours?"

"I be not ready to accuse this Otis of creating corpses, but he has some poor ideas about the ownership of silver."

"And even poorer judgment, making comments like that to the gardener."

"Aye. So let's go fishing. Pretend to Burnside that George just spilled his guts and see what topics of conversation Otis gets most flustered about. Trade up some info, so to speak."

"Might as well. With everyone else in the division chasing legitimate leads, about all we have are fishing holes."

"Right. Make our own leads." Tom walked on in frowning rumination.

"Anything bothering you, Tommy?"

"Aye, now ye mention it. How good are ye at pulling out cactus stickers?"

Heldt Museum is never busy in midsummer, but something nearby must have been. Every parking space on the block was filled. Tom finally spotted one on the far side, wrenched the wheel and sent his Bug into a clumsy about-face. "Love these impromptu U-turns. Keeps me in practice." He backed into a narrow space. It took him three zigs and zags.

Joe slid out and locked his door. "Any particular way you want to approach this?"

"No. Just act terribly hurt and disappointed that Otis should be holding out on us like this, and we'll feel around for what he might be hiding. Look on the bright side, Jose, me lad. At least George's name doesn't have a B in it. Crosses him off our list of murder suspects."

"Yeah. The bright side." Joe took two steps and stopped in midstride, an unwise thing to do on a busy street. "Pronounce his last name, Tommy."

"Varendes."

"That's Americanese. Now listen to it in Spanish. Barendes."

Tom stared at him. "Mother Murphy's earmuffs! Our Lawrence Banks might well hear that and mistake the V for a B."

"And in the shock and stress of his injury couldn't recall the alien word. His garbling might have been the inability to remember an unfamiliar three-syllable name. Varendes isn't common in Spanish."

"But George denied knowing him."

Joe continued on across the street as a car whizzed past, its driver scowling at him. "George recognized half the name and most of the description. We should have pushed him harder on how well he knew that Larry, and any background he had on him."

"How could we've slipped up like that?! I was hungry, that was why. Argh!"

Joe entered the big arching front gates of Heldt Museum and stopped so fast Tom bumped into him. Burnside stood in a glassed-in office to the right, arguing violently with someone on the telephone. He nodded. He shook his head. He raised his hand and patted the air as if to mollify the caller.

Tom ducked into the outer office to the left. A perplexed young man half rose in the receptionist's chair. "I must hear Mr. Burnside's conversation!" Tom snatched the phone off the hook and punched the lighted extension button.

"Too late." Joe watched Burnside cradle the receiver. "Hear anything at all?"

"Not even male or female. Ye suppose it's our cactus-wrestler?"

"Inside chance." Joe started across the entranceway. Burnside saw him coming and disappeared into his inner office. The glass door was locked. Joe turned away.

Tommy jogged out the front gate. Mrs. Schumacher appeared in her outer office.

Joe ran over and stuck his head in the door. "We have to talk to Otis Burnside and his door's locked."

"As far as I'm concerned, it can stay locked." She looked even stiffer and gaunter in a severely tailored business suit than she had in blue jeans.

Joe picked up the phone and glared menacingly at the receptionist. "Burnside's extension."

Timidly the young man poked a button. Beeps. No answer.

Schumacher planted herself in front of him. "Mr. Martinez . . . No. Ramirez . . . Rodriguez. That's it. Otis is probably on his way to an appointment. He's seriously in arrears with his craft festival preparations. I'd appreciate it if you gentlemen would leave him alone."

"The fair isn't for three months yet."

"Do you realize how little time that is? Everyone knows an investigation such as yours stretches on for months, so don't give me any song and dance about the need to consume hours of Otis' time just now."

"You're saying this museum won't cooperate with us?"

"I still run this asylum. If you need information, ask me. Let Burnside do the job he gets paid for."

"Mrs. Schumacher, I . . ."

Tom came jogging in from the front gate again, panting. "He left the back way all afluster. The most I saw was his tail lights disappearing up Seventh."

Schumacher sighed. "If you two must pursue your investigations pell-mell, make an appointment with Mr. Burnside through the receptionist here." She turned on her heel and marched away into her inner office.

Joe gave the young man the evil eye again. "Appointments. Where's Mr. Burnside going now?"

The fellow thumbed through a plastic-bound calendar. "Nothing written in for this afternoon."

Joe peered over his shoulder to confirm the conspicuous blank space.

Tommy shrugged and led the way outside. "We can chase him down. Or we can go find George and play the same game—pretend Burnside spilled all and see what we can get."

Joe grunted. "I have a good mind to put the word out on our Mr. Burnside."

"Let our stalwart boys in blue citywide find him and haul him to the pokey? To what end?"

"Let him cool his heels in the anthill awhile to soften him up. Too busy, she says." Joe strolled out the gate.

"Might well have the opposite effect; being arrested in the street by uniformed officers might just drive him so deep we'll get nothing at all useful from him. Let's dig him out quietly and try to cajole him into being helpful."

Joe studied the burning sky for want of anything better to look at. When in doubt, look up. "We should split up, probably. George said something about planting roses at Thompsons. I'll check that out. If he's there I'll call you. And I'll find out from the Botanical Garden which Rackham."

"Let's send some simple souls in blue out to watch George's and Otis' homes. Surely, they have to go home eventually."

East over the Superstitions, thunderheads were building themselves to towering heights. A few less impressive cloudbanks were stacking themselves above the Estrellas to the south. The thunderstorm season was starting early this year.

Why not? Everything else was out of whack.

Wet T-Shirt

When they took the trouble to plant these mansions on the sheer face of Camelback Mountain, why didn't they go all the way and bury the power lines? Joe considered that little enigma as he paused halfway up the endless flight of stairs from the parking area to the Thompson estate. True, the lines weren't conspicuous, but you could see them out there if you knew where to look. Tom's Irish luck qualified him as a leprechaun, all right; he was probably still at his desk exercising nothing more than his dialing finger while Joe scaled peaks. Next time, Joe would think twice about splitting up to chase wild geese. His bad leg was about ready to give out.

A thunderstorm – one of those black beauties the desert specializes in – poised nearly overhead. The wind shifted directions and temperatures; a cold blast hit him. It felt good on his sweaty face. He started climbing again.

He was near the top when lightning struck the rocks less than half a mile away. He heard pebbles—or perhaps boulders—rattle somewhere. He climbed faster. The only vehicle in the lot besides his own was Varendes' battered white pickup. Maybe no one else was home. As he topped out, he heard the hum of an air conditioner in an upstairs window.

To the west another of those white lightning bolts flicked down. The transformer beyond the house flared orange flames. Instantly the cooler hum fell silent. Thunder clapped and shook the whole mountain.

He broke into a trot as the first drops heralded the hard and beating rain to follow. He ducked under the patio roof and turned to watch the awesome sky. These violent storms were impressive enough on flat ground. Here on the mountainside they were just plain scary.

The patio was half roofed, half open. The dull orange bricks in the patterned floor glistened dark red where the rain could reach them. Joe followed along under the overhang until protection ended and the rain drummed in front of him.

He saw George beyond the pool, getting absolutely soaked. The rain slashed down now in fast zinging sheets. George didn't seem to notice. Doggedly he chipped and dug at rose plantings along a trellised wall. A wheelbarrow, blankets, and a bag of peat lay strewn about him, getting just as wet as he.

Should Joe kill two birds with one stone and ask

George about the Lawrence that Bernice used to date? Or should he wait and let Tommy tackle him? Better wait. Tom might well have found Burnside by now. Once in a while—once in a great while—Joe regretted not installing a radio or car phone in his Midget. He could use it now to compare notes with Tom.

Joe finally decided he was Sanforized. . . . What could a little rain do to him? He stepped out into the downpour and crossed to the gardener.

"George. George! Señor Varendes?"

The man wheeled wild-eyed and stared at Joe, so panic-stricken he actually turned white. By degrees he gathered his wits back in and returned his attentions to the rosebushes.

"Sorry I startled you. Joe Rodriguez, remember?"

"Yeah. Sure. Botanical Garden this morning. Wha' can I do for you?"

"Real frog-strangler, this rain. Terrible time to be planting roses."

"Yeah. Colder'n fish and toads, but I gotta get this done. Other stuff to do yet. Mrs. Thompson, she always has lahss for me to do." Cold indeed; George's hands were shaking. He stretched out a leg to stomp loose dirt. The rosebush waggled precariously. His shirt and pants pasted themselves tightly against his skin.

"So you mentioned. We're trying to find Otis Burnside. He has no appointments on his calendar; his wife and secretary don't know where he is; we're checking with friends and relatives. Think you can help us?" Joe changed his mind. Yes, he would ask George about Banks.

"Ain' seen him lately. Nope." George flicked his shovel around to tamp with the handle and flipped it back to digging mode. He should have been a baton twirler.

"Do you know any favorite hangouts of his? Places he might go when he's upset or wants to think things through? Bars, clubs, that sort of thing?"

"We never drink together, him and me." Dig, dig, dig.

"Mmmm. He received a phone call early this afternoon just before he disappeared. Would you happen to . . ."

Joe should have seen it coming, but he didn't—not in time. George was catching him with his guard down. Joe's mind boggled instantly—with rage at having been caught unprepared, and with caution; the swimming pool was right behind him. He must not step back too far. He grabbed for his gun with his good hand as he raised his right arm to block the blow, but the shovel came at his head faster than a striking snake, faster than he could move. All he saw was that wet, steel blade coming at his face. He didn't really even feel it hit.

"Ginia, bring me some brandy too." It sounded like Bernice. "I need warming up."

Ginia's voice babbled from miles away.

"Aw, Ginia, you hardnose." Yep. Bernice.

Rain splashed against the bricks, drummed on the patio overhang, joined with thunderclaps into a cacophony of confusing noise. He was sprawled out on the patio beneath the overhang and Bernice sat cross-legged beside him.

She grinned amiably. "Ginia was right. Bet she knew you were waking up before you did."

His brain rebelled against the noise and the headache and refused to try to sort this mess out. George was getting away, might even have reached his truck by now. Joe struggled to get up, to go after George, and this disrespectful child-woman kept holding him down. She was screaming at him. The words finally penetrated into his howling, pounding brain.

". . . anywhere, you big dope. Don't you understand? You were *dead* five minutes ago!"

He let his heavy head fall back on the sofa pillow or whatever that was under him. She was still rattling on like a machine gun.

"You Mexican lummox. See? Now it's bleeding again. Darnit, I get it all squared away and you decide to run laps." She poked at his head with some sort of rag; her facade of casual good cheer had shattered. Her face was knotted into worry lines as if he were a beloved brother. His breastbone hurt so much he could barely breathe.

Ginia's bulk hovered at his other side. "This 'ere is for when you feel up to it." Balancing a brandy snifter, she settled herself cautiously beside his elbow. "I generally frown on spirits, Mr. Rodriguez, but there is a place for 'em. And you are definitely at the place."

He managed with help to jack himself to sitting. Maybe he'd think better sitting up. Stabbing pain shot through his chest. He drew his legs up, flopped his elbows across his knees and sat tricornered, sipping brandy. He was soaked to the skin, wetter than rain could make him.

So was Bernice. Her faded T-shirt, lettered with I LIKE SCHOOL BEST—WHEN IT'S CLOSED, clung to her.

The situation dawned by degrees. George's shovel had knocked him into the swimming pool and she had jumped in after him. He was slow to notice the puddle of vomit nearby. He knew, and now Bernice knew, that mouth-to-mouth resuscitation does that. You put in a couple breaths and can almost count on getting something back.

Dead five minutes ago. And he wasn't sharp enough to see it coming. George. His ears burned.

He knew without asking but he asked anyway. "Do you have phone service?"

Bernice shook her head. "Ginia tried already. And the power outage must be general, at least here on the mountain. If it's only our house, a burglar alarm goes off downtown and they send out some fuzz. No fuzz. Except you, of course."

"Lightning zapped your transformer. It's going to be awhile. Look, I have to reach Tom before George flies the coop."

"Forget it." Her voice, once sharp and sarcastic, flowed soft and warm. It contrasted with her shivering. He was chilled too. The rain was abating, but the cold wind was not.

"Where's Mrs. Thompson?"

"Mom went to a bridge game this afternoon with the girls. You know, fifty-year-old, 200-pound girls. She won't come up the hill until the storm quits."

Ginia looked ready for brandy herself. She

wagged her head. "The way Bernice was shrieking through the house, I thought doomsday was here. 'That Indian cop is moccasins-up in our swimming pool!' she yells. And you'd be dead forever if she didn't know zackly what to do. We fished you out and she cranked up your motor again with that CPR thing. Took thirty years off my life. But there ain' no phone cause we tried to get help, and there ain' no power, and there ain' no way anybody's going down them stairs with this lightning and all. I ain' going I don' care who's dead, and I won' let either of you."

Joe now saw clearly the real power behind the Thompson throne.

The two women argued for five minutes over what to do next and Bernice lost. They sat him at the kitchen table just inside the sliding glass doors and Ginia busied herself making hot chocolate. Bernice disappeared and returned moments later wearing dry clothes. They didn't cling.

She threw some clothes across the back of a chair. "These are my father's. The sweater's half orlon, but boy is it warm. Come on, change."

While he emptied his pockets out on the table, she set his wallet on end and fanned it open. He laid his gun on the table. Before he could tell her hands off, she picked it up and snapped the cylinder out. He watched rapt as she dismantled his gun using a kitchen knife as her only tool. He made another mental note—she was left-handed.

"Go shooting much?"

She shook her head. "Used to. Skeet too. But I got bored with it." She glanced at him. "It's not polite to stare."

"Just admiring competence. Sorry. Where'd you learn resuscitation?"

"My father had a mild heart attack last year. That's what triggered his Sports Hero jag. Fitness. And I've always kind of liked medicine. First aid. So I took the Red Cross course. The CPR card came with the package. Just the ticket if Dad drops over. I really would appreciate it if you'd quit staring at me and put those dry clothes on."

Carefully he touched the lump on the side of his head. It was growing, and his headache was more than keeping pace. "I'm still not thinking straight. I don't understand you. I was certain you didn't have the concern of a goldfish. Now this."

"Don't feel like the Lone Ranger. Or Tonto, as the case may be." She blotted the spring dry with a facial tissue. "Sometimes I surprise myself. Impulsive. Most of what I do is on impulse. So don't accidentally mistake me for a noble person."

Her voice dropped a notch. "I was upstairs reading when the lights went out and the cooler died, so I wandered over to the window. I watched you come jogging across our yard—old Preacher Rodriguez—and I hated your guts. Then George did his little number on you, and you were in real trouble, and I couldn't get downstairs fast enough. People are weird, right?"

"Right. Would you have hurried so hard if it had been a total stranger in your pool?" Joe paused. "Or your mother?"

She opened her mouth and closed it again, swallowing her flip answer. She held his eye. "I don't know. I hope so."

"What was that business at the dog pound? You ran."

She glanced at him guiltily and shrugged. "You get along real well with your kids. I can tell because they swarm all over you and you let them."

"They're annoying sometimes, but all kids are."

"The thought struck me then that Dad never once let me sit on his knee like that and put an arm around him. It never occurred to him, I don't think, and it never occurred to me. Daddies don't do that. Daddies go to work all day. And . . . I don't know. I got to yearning, wishing Dad had snuggled me like that. Wishing he went along to pick out a dog, or go to the movies or anything, y'know? And it got away from me."

"You miss the fathering, but you took a first aid course to save him?"

"I told you people are weird. Meet one of the weirdest."

Ginia plunked mugs of hot chocolate in front of them. He should be welcoming the warm and sugary pick-me-up, but the aroma was mildly nauseating. Everything was mildly nauseating. Ginia wiggled a finger at Bernice. "He don' need help changing his clothes. Go file your comic books or something."

Bernice's mood shifted instantly. "What a spoilsport. I'll open up Tavery's room for him. That way he can take a nap and won't have to climb stairs." She stood up. "Understand I'm busy, or I'd love to stick around. I enjoy a good comedy show." She left the kitchen singing, "It's Howdy Doody Time."

Except for the headache, and the fact that he got dizzy every time he turned his head, he was doing pretty well. He paused by the pool to admire the clear morning sky. Dead fifteen hours ago. It still wasn't really sinking in. Was he dead as in pulse-and-respiration-both-gone, or just no-respiration? He never had got that straight, not that it really mattered.

The shovel protruded from a rosebush where George had thrown it. Joe hefted it and started poking around the flower bed, pursuing a hunch.

"Begorra, lad! What be ye thinking of?!"

Joe turned very slowly to watch Tom come jogging around the far end of the pool. "Good morning. How many times have you told me that the use of 'begorra' is an ethnic stereotype to be avoided?"

"You're not even supposed to be up and about." Tom snatched the shovel out of Joe's hand.

"Look, Tommy, I'm all ri–"

"Jose, me obstinate partner, ye were very nearly rendered permanently posthumous last night." He tilted Joe's head slightly for a better look. "Argh! Clobbered three shades of purple and ye try to load sixteen tons. You're daft. Meself will operate the shovel. Go sit down. What be we excavating?"

Joe settled himself cautiously into a lawn chair and felt much better immediately. "You and Ginia. Together you'd rule the world. Ginia said that Bernice went out last night to call you."

"Aye." Tom leaned casually on the shovel. "Rock slide blocked the road below the parking area, so she couldn't take your car, and hers is in the shop. Bernice had to walk most the way down the mountain to find a working phone."

"How'd George get his truck over the slide?"

"Didn't. Got it half way over before it hung up completely. He walked too. Anyway, Bernice called 911 and they called me. What do ye want dug up here so badly?"

"That rosebush, for starters. Drive cleared now?"

"Aye. Got the street department on it first thing this morning. Mayhap ye heard the front-end loader."

"Heard something down there, yeah."

Tom hacked at the dirt as he talked. He was no gardener. "The way Bernice described your condition, ye were in no immediate danger. Pulse, pupils, the whole shebang. She's halfway a doctor. So I gave her a handy talkie and drove her back up as far as the rockslide. If ye turned for the worse, she was to radio me and we'd send a chopper in."

"Thanks for waiting till I got worse."

"Don't speak sarcastically, me beloved compatriot. Meself was all in favor of lofting ye in the wind straight to Asimoto in emergency. But the department's in this money crunch, no doubt ye noticed. I can just see the lieutenant's face, should he come home from Colorado and we hand him the bill for a chopper. Hallo! What's this?"

"Burnside, I suspect." Joe stood up. He couldn't feel less like standing up. He walked over.

Tom scraped and gouged and scratched the dirt off a knee. No, it was an elbow. He raised the end of the arm on his shovel. It was a left arm, very stiff, and on the hand an elaborate silver and turquoise wedding band.

Tom nodded sagely. "Logical. Ye didn't actually accuse George of snuffing a life, I trust."

"No, that was his guilty conscience talking. He might be our sniper, but I rather doubt it. From the way he acted, I think this was his first."

"Ye only need one, ye know, to qualify."

A course, throaty gasp behind Joe startled him. He turned and nearly spun out. Bernice was staring at the hole in the rose bed, paralyzed. Joe stepped in front of her to break her gaze, stiff-armed her two steps backward and turned her around. Her face drained white. She wrapped around him. The top of her head just brushed his chin. He snugged his arms in around her shoulders; he owed her a hug at the very least.

She shuddered all over and whispered, "Who is it?"

"Burnside, tentatively. Did you see him come up here yesterday? George acting suspicious? Anything?"

Her head on his breast gave a negative shake.

"Any idea why or how this happened? Hear arguments?"

"No. He was a mouse. A crab. But why kill him? Why put him . . . there?"

"No dogs here to dig him up. He could have gone undetected for years, as deep as he is. Did you see George come to work yesterday afternoon?"

"No. I was reading until the power went out. I wasn't looking. The air conditioner was running; I didn't hear anything. I'd still be reading if the lights hadn't quit. Take me inside."

She was glassy-eyed and weak-kneed. He walked

to the patio door into the kitchen, the closest route inside. Behind them Tom was talking Americanese into his handy talkie. The place would be swarming with cops shortly, and Maynard Rust's lab crew. They would spend hours with Bernice, with Ginia, with himself. It was just beginning.

She stopped and unwrapped her arm from his waist. "I'm okay now. I'm going upstairs. Send Ginia up to get me when you need something." She started inside and paused in the door. "And Joe? When Mom gets home, please don't tell her, uh, you know—the dead part. That you were dead for awhile. Please? Not anything about that part." She shuffled off and disappeared into the gloom.

The Crab's Scam

The late Otis Burnside had a good eye for decor. In addition to the spacious desk, the roomy chair, the woodtone file cabinets, his office boasted a tasteful coffee table and an overstuffed couch. Joe appreciated the comfort as he slouched across the sofa with his legs sprawled out. Gretchen and Doug were packing their bags, having just given the Burnside office the usual tech going-over.

Tom sat in Burnside's chair, exploring the desk drawers. "Nothing out of the ordinary. Something of a disappointment. Meself was hoping for some sort of nippy little tidbit."

"Like porn pix, sex toys, and calendars. You men are all alike." Gretchen picked up the wife's photo on the desk. "Wholesome. His old lady looks so wholesome it's nauseating."

"Acts and talks wholesome, as well." Tom closed a drawer. "Harry says she's so middle-class she buys all her appliances from Sears." He looked at Joe. "Jose, lad, won't ye go home for a couple days and sleep it off? Ye look like death in a doodoo bin."

"Funny. I feel vivacious."

Gretchen stopped at the door on her way out and patted Joe's shoulder. "Be a good boy and listen to your uncle Tommy. Tommy knows best." She snorted. "At least that's what he keeps telling me." She jogged out behind Doug.

"One of her finest virtues—she recognizes me brilliance." Tom sat back in the chair, expansive, relaxed. "Ah, that Otis knew how to work. One steno served both Burnside and Schumacher. The male receptionist out front handles all appointments so as to be able to coordinate the two of them when needed. He has no idea what sent Burnside scurrying out the door yesterday afternoon, nor where he went."

"Does he recognize the name or face of Lawrence Banks?"

"No, I tried him three or four ways on that. And no connection between Banks and Burnside that we can find."

"What does the receptionist know about George?"

"Only what he ought—that Varendes be the gardener and handyman, good for pickup work, and Burnside fancied using him now and again. He seemed open and comfortable about it all."

"How about connections between Schumacher

and Varendes and Banks?"

"Meself was hoping that might be a fertile line of endeavor but so far, nothing."

Joe tried to nod and quit instantly. "Harley and Turk find anything interesting about Banks' friends and acquaintances?"

"Not yet, and tis frustrating, Harley says. Banks was as blah a buddy as you'd ever get stuck with. Burned weeds with a chum now and then, an occasional drink. Never close to anyone."

"Girlfriends? He was handsome enough to do a pretty good Adonis impersonation."

"No one regular. Mostly one-nighters. Between 'em Harley and Turk interviewed nine ladies."

"Jilted lover decked him and a cute chick misidentified as his latest throb. Jealous rage."

"Harley says they worked on that some, but it's not at all promising. None of the girls was much hung up on him, especially after they slept with him."

"Has Mel been looking at the possibility the killer was deliberately after Mouse?"

"Ye mean revenge? Or a love triangle?"

"Why not? Young, cute, perky."

"And no boyfriends. Nor any convicted felons promising retribution. Most of Robbery looked at that angle."

Joe still got dizzy every time he turned his head. He kept it as stationary as possible. "And no leads on that Robert Hawkins. I asked Hennie to run the alias 'Loop' through her machine. No hits. She tried the French 'Loupe' and got three makes, all political activists, two of them Canadians. Nothing near

Banks' description. That's dead-ended."

Tom put his feet up on the desk, cautiously at first, and pulled his cigarettes. "Whilst yourself was trotting briskly up the mountain to find George, I happened to be passing Berendsi's, so I stopped by. That Mrs. Cutter who works Saturdays on the furniture side was no help whatever. Dimmer by a good bit than Lu Ella. Berendsi still looks like a promising candidate."

"Berendsi's been an object of robbery division scrutiny for some time now; did he know Mouse?"

"Pete says no." Tom lit up and squirmed deeper into the encompassing chair. "This Burnside has no alibi, either. During the hour in question he was out talking to people, theoretically. But the receptionist has no names on the calendar, and Burnside, of course, died before giving us anything that would make or break his whereabouts."

"My fault. I should've established that first instead of sidetracking into silver. I hate starting an interview with, 'Where were you on the night of?' "

"A profitable sidetrack, from his reactions."

Joe rubbed his face. Just past 3:30 and he felt as tired as if it were midnight. He had died yesterday right about this time. He sat up straighter for fear of falling asleep. "Brent Sommers—what have we gathered on him?"

"Chen and Harry worked on that. Joe College. Big Man on Campus, or so he thought. Intramural jock, mostly volleyball, but not good enough for varsity anything. President of the drinking club in his fraternity. Escorted the homecoming queen not once but two years running. Average scholastically."

"Nothing shady?"

Tom wagged his head. "Couple speeding tickets in the last few years. Totaled his car once. Divorced twice already and working on his third. Hasn't held any job more than eighteen months. Always moves up when he takes a new position. Ambitious, impressed with money in any shape or form."

"What kind of future would he be planning with an art museum?"

Tom shrugged. "He's one of three assistant directors. So he has a 33 percent chance of . . ."

Someone was knocking at the door.

Tom swung his legs to the floor and sat erect. "Come in."

A gray-haired lady stepped in cautiously. "Mr. Burnside?"

Tom hesitated only the barest moment. He switched into flawless Americanese. "What can I do for you?"

The lady looked at Joe. "Oh, excuse me. The receptionist was out of his office. I'll come back later."

"Not at all. I was just leaving." Joe stood up. "Pleasure doing business with you, sir." He crossed to the desk and extended his hand.

Tom stood up to shake. He hunched over a bit, perhaps from long years of sitting at desks. It was beautiful. "Have a safe trip home."

"Thank you." Joe smiled pleasantly at the lady and ambled out, closing the door gently behind him. He sprinted through the outer office and across to Schumacher's side. The receptionist was coming out of Schumacher's inner office as Joe bolted in. Joe reached the man's desk, punched the intercom open and usurped the chair. The exertion left him intensely dizzy. Through the painful, thumping fog he listened to the conversation in Burnside's office as Tom opened the other end of the line.

The lady was speaking. ". . . over in Scottsdale. You remember Mrs. Hilts."

Tom grunted noncommittally. "Mrs. Lewiston, I believe in speaking openly and clearly, so there's no misunderstanding. I assume this lady you mention told you that."

"She said you're very careful in your dealings. Discreet."

"Discretion and clarity are two different things. Please describe exactly what you seek so I can tell precisely whether I can help you."

"You know. Dead pawn. Old pieces. The kind of pieces that make the best long-range investment. Like you sold Helen Hilts."

"That silverwork was unique. One of a kind. You mean, perhaps, something similar."

"Of course." The feminine voice sounded flustered.

"Just what did Mrs. Hilts tell you? You seem to have scant regard for quality."

"Hardly!" The flustered voice took on an incensed edge. "I have a very high regard for quality. That's why I came. Helen assures me that the pieces you provide are of the very highest quality. She had some of them independently appraised, you know."

Joe knew what he'd say next, but he had no way

of communicating it to Tom. He felt a rustle by his shoulder. Dr. Schumacher was standing there.

Tom: "I don't always have prime pieces available."

The lady: "But you said on the phone yesterday morning that you did."

Schumacher's arm lashed out and punched the intercom. Silence. She glowered black as a raven at no one in particular, turned her back on Joe and wandered over to the window.

"How much do you know about Burnside's scam, Doctor?"

"Stay out of it. This has nothing to do with your homicide investigation."

"I'll wager it does. And it has everything to do with Pete Mark's department. Or possibly bunco. You can sit down and talk to me now or have a whole police department on your back."

The phone rang. Joe was sitting in the receptionist's chair. He answered it. "Heldt Museum."

"Is Detective Tom Flaherty there, please?"

"I'll connect you, Mr. Wallace. And don't be surprised if he sounds funny—not quite like himself. Mrs. Schumacher, what's Burnside's extension?"

Sour as green apples, she punched a button. Joe stayed on.

Tom: "Yes?"

Harry Wallace: "You sure this is Tom Flaherty?"

Tom: "Absolutely. I grew up with him, you know."

Harry: "Yeah, it's you. We picked up George Varendes fifteen minutes ago. Does Joe want the attempted murder rap on him as well as the Burnside killing, or just assaulting an officer? Hey, was that Joe answering the phone?"

Tom: "That's good news. Yes. Lay it all on. Every little bit helps. I shall connect you with my personal secretary." Tom's end died.

Joe spoke. "Harry? I got downgraded from partner to secretary."

"Thought that was you. Why'd he sound so funny?"

"He's practicing to be an impressionist. Might book into Vegas with the winter season."

"Not unless he gets a whole lot better. Your man finally showed up at his house and we were waiting. No resistance. Forgot English."

"Let him stew in a closet, but not the torture chamber. We'll be down in a few minutes. Got a pot boiling here. Thanks, Harry." Joe cradled the phone. "Dr. Schumacher, shall we slip into something comfortable—your office, perhaps—and talk turkey?"

She sighed heavily. "I suppose it's inevitable. No visitors, Ralph, except his partner, and no calls."

Joe got up and held her door for her.

She wandered lackadaisically over to her own desk and flopped into a chair every bit as comfortable as Burnside's. She looked as bone-weary as Joe felt. "Otis had been acting a bit peculiarly for some months. Furtive. But I had no idea the extent of what was happening. I scheduled a closed board meeting for 10 tomorrow morning. I hoped to present our predicament to the board before it leaked out."

"What is 'it' exactly?" Joe chose not the most

comfortable chair left, but the nearest. He sat.

"I'm not altogether certain yet. Apparently Otis was selling off our classic pieces and replacing them with inferior pieces, then doctoring the records to cover the switch. He had free rein with the silver collection, as you know."

"How did you catch on?"

"Yesterday morning I decided to check personally to see that inventory sheets, the photo record, accession cards, etc., were all in order. If the worst happened and a theft succeeded, we could identify missing pieces instantly and perhaps find some of them. Some of the oldest, most valued pieces were represented by bright new cards. White cards instead of aging yellow cards. Not just one or two but many. Dozens."

"Don't you keep your inventory on computer?"

"We maintain complete inventories in both forms. If we had abandoned the card system, I never would have noticed the irregularity."

"So he would destroy all record of a museum piece, sell the piece, and then replace it with a lesser piece, pocketing the difference as profit? The museum records show nothing amiss?"

"Considerable profit." She still looked crisp and efficient, but no longer did she appear invulnerable. "The captain goes down with the ship. We depend primarily on donations for new material. Important material. This should successfully dry up any future gifts. An invaluable collection—a priceless collection—flown to the four winds." Her sad eyes met Joe's for the first time. "Mr. Burnside successfully destroyed our past and our future in one stroke."

'Where were you yesterday from 1 o'clock on?"

"I can't express my disgust and bitterness. Otis ravaged this museum for personal gain. But I wouldn't murder him."

"That doesn't answer my question."

"No place that would provide what you would call an ironclad alibi. I looked over the temporary exhibit at the art museum."

"Stop by Brent's office?"

"No. I only wanted to see the traveling collection. Frankly, I wanted to be familiar with it, in case they ever think of divesting themselves of any part of it."

"And did you . ."

Tom burst in. "Did ye hear, Joe?"

"Only to the point of, 'But you said you did on the phone yesterday.' And I talked to Harry."

"Ah. Then we best go downtown, eh?"

Joe almost nodded. "Dr. Schumacher, the police, the media, the whole world are going to jump on this sooner or later. I advise you, let it be sooner. Call Pete Marks in right now. Don't try to wait until morning. The quicker you air your laundry, the better you yourself will smell."

"I'll take your suggestion under advisement." She sat quietly. She did not wish them good-bye.

Tom spent the whole trip to headquarters regaling Joe about his scam with Mrs. Lewiston. Joe listened with half an ear. He was piecing things together, in spite of himself. If only his head would quit pounding, this puzzle might fall into place. Tom parked in a center-lot slot.

Joe climbed out slowly and leaned a moment on the roof staring beyond Tom. "Burnside is taller than five eight."

Tom leaned too. "Aye, but not hunched over the way he usually moved."

"And did you notice Schumacher's doctoral diploma on her office wall?"

"Not to speak of."

"Vale is her middle name."

"And her Christian name?"

"Brenda. Brenda Schumacher."

Another B.

Skateboard Fever

In Homicide there is an interrogation room affectionately called the torture chamber. Tastefully decorated in shades of pale blue, sienna, and pink, it is scientifically designed to relax, to ease hostility, to promote loquaciousness. Tom, the best interrogator in Phoenix, worked miracles of information extraction there.

Today Tom was thwarted. The lawyer accompanying George Varendes took one look at the room, realized its function, and refused to permit his client to enter. And so they sat in a gray and cheerless room of the Old School.

It didn't ease Tom's frustration that the lawyer had laughed at his incipient moustache and wished him luck growing anything visible. It didn't ease Joe's frustration that the lawyer assiduously ignored him. And that every time Tom asked a question, he warned

George, "You don't have to answer."

Now, apparently, the lawyer figured he had achieved a useful level of frustration. He leaned tête-à-tête in a deal-making attitude toward Tom. "Look, Flaherty. The Burnside thing is circumstantial. You'll get a manslaughter out of it if you're lucky, and I doubt you'll get that much. All you have with Rodriguez here is assault and battery . . ."

"Like blazes, Hanson!" Joe exploded. "I was clinically dead, with two witnesses to prove it. Attempted murder, at least. And Hickey is toying with the notion of going for murder two. If those women hadn't been there and known exactly what to do, it would've stayed murder."

The lawyer half rose in his chair. "You're deliberately trying to intimidate my client. You're going—"

"Ye know," Tom injected casually, "that should be an interesting precedent. Joe was killed. And just because he failed to remain dead hardly rules out murder. We'd love to see our names in all the lawbooks someday."

Wide-eyed, George burst out, "I didn' wanna kill you. I got scared, thass all." As his fear built, his English disintegrated.

"Shut up, Varendes," snarled the lawyer.

Joe pressed him. "Then why'd you run off and leave me soaking?"

"Porque tenia miedo." George brought his voice under a bit better control. It dropped a notch. "Lo siento. Por Dios, lo siento." He was shaking enough to make his folding chair creak.

"No Spanish!" his lawyer snapped. "You don't say anything. They're trying to scare you. There *is* precedent, and it's favorable."

"Porque no podemos hablar Español, Hanson? Porque tu no lo entiendes?" Joe asked, as he glanced at Tom. Tom closed his eyes in the barest of affirmative gestures.

George's eyes darted from Tom to the lawyer to Joe. You could read it on his face: he was picking the person most sympathetic to his cause, and that person, not too surprisingly, was Joe. The man he had nearly killed was also his own kind, a brother who would understand in either language.

"What you do for me, I tell you 'bout Otis?"

The lawyer beat time on the table with a stabbing finger. "The reason I am here, Varendes, is to protect your best interests. That means you depend upon my knowledge of the law and its safeguards. And I'm telling you right now, shut up!"

"I don' trust you no more 'n I trust him." George dipped his head toward Tom. Tom deliberately scrunched down to appear as inconspicuous as possible.

"Mir'!" Joe turned his head and pointed to his black and green knot. "I'm mad enough to bite the heads off snakes and you can't blame me. Even if you didn't mean to put me down, you messed me up royally. I'm not going to smile and call you compadre, but I believe you when you say you didn't mean to. I'll trust your word and you trust mine. We make a deal, and that's how it'll be. All right?"

The lawyer started shouting in earnest, but George didn't seem to hear him. He studied Joe closely. "You let me off for hitting you, I tell you everything I know 'bout Otis."

"Deal."

"No! Self-incrimination!" But the lawyer had already lost.

Joe shifted into Spanish and received willing replies. Tom might not understand the conversation, but he was surely basking in the pure joy of watching Hanson's frustration. George relaxed a bit, relatively speaking, and bared his soul, safe from prying Anglo ears.

An hour later George returned to his cell pending arraignment and bail, the lawyer promised worlds of legal mayhem, and Joe and Tom flipped a penny. Heads, dinner at the Wienie Barn. Tails, dinner at the Extraburger. Extraburger won. They flipped again on the front step and Joe's car won over Tom's. He slid behind the wheel and paused a moment until his head cleared.

The Midget bobbed as Tom hopped in and slammed his door. "Glory to the queen! I wanted ye to switch tongues and didn't know how to tell ye. I knew it'd loosen him up; a veritable verbal laxative. Did ye watch Hanson's face? He woulda stabbed his darling grandmamma to shut ye up."

Joe opened his door and climbed out. "You drive." Tom stood up in the little open car and stepped from seat to seat. He plopped to sitting, tangling briefly in the gearshift. Joe crawled into the passenger side, scrunched into the corner, and closed his eyes. It'd been a long, hard day of tedium and the constant need to remain alert.

"I'm sore tempted to trot ye right over to Mays this minute."

"Don't bother. It's Lee's day off and I don't cotton to that Hausmann."

"Look at me."

Joe opened his eyes.

Tom was studying him suspiciously. "Your pupils are normal—or you'd just have to cotton to Hausmann. Tell me what George knows about Otis." He torched off the motor and they were on their way.

"Apparently Burnside went out of his way to meet George at Thompsons. Deliberate. Spoke to him, nice to him. Got him a couple odd jobs that paid very well."

"Think he salted the kitty? Added some funds of his own to make the odd jobs look even better?"

"Quite possibly. Even George sees now that Burnside was buttering him up, and lavishly. Eventually Burnside let the cat out. He wanted George's help in stealing Royce Howard."

Tom whistled. "The whole collection? What made Burnside think George was his man?"

"Interesting. Beneath his humble exterior, Burnside was a real conniver. He appealed to George's nationalism and liberal political views. Burnside's pitch was that Mrs. Thompson's collection represents the very best of Mexican and Indian craftsmanship and is too good to lie moldering in some rich capitalist's upstairs room. It belongs to the world."

"Ah!" Tom had a bad habit of flapping about wildly while driving. Both hands left the wheel briefly. You just don't do that with an MG. "I heard Lawrence Banks' name bandied about here and there amongst the gibberish. How did he fit in?"

"As far as either George or I can tell, not at all."

"Then Mouse and Banks are a whole different matter." Tom pulled into the Extraburger lot. The speed bump made Joe's head pound. "On second thought, not necessarily. Burnside would tell George not a datum more than he absolutely had to; Banks might fit in, unbeknownst to George. Did George agree to go along?"

"I'm pretty sure he did, although he claimed he didn't. He has keys to portions of the burglar alarm system because he often came up to Thompsons when no one was home. Burnside knew the interior layout but not the daily routine, especially Ginia's. George did, to an extent. Actually, George didn't stand to get much out of it. He thought the loot would go to the museum."

They parked near the door. Tom bounced out and stood a moment studying his own reflection in the fender. "Why? With all the silver in the world, why would Burnside wish to lift Royce Howard?"

"He didn't have all the silver in the world, not anymore. He had a lucrative business rolling, and a shortage of top quality merchandise. I'd guess he'd let George help him transfer Royce Howard from Thompsons to the museum, then unknown to George sell it piece by piece as he had been doing all along. George would assume it was safely tucked away and Burnside wouldn't even have to replace it. Hundred percent profit."

"Ahh. Which leaves but one question. Why did George send Burnside up to bug Saint Peter?"

"Panicked. George had already learned by

chance, gossiping with Ginia, that a flock of cops showed up at that pool party. When we talked to him at the Botanical Garden, he thought we knew more than we were letting on. He figured we were onto them and called Burnside to warn him, get him to bail out." Joe crawled out to standing reluctantly.

"Ah." Tom headed toward the door. "No doubt that was he on the phone when we walked into the museum. George confronted Burnside personally at some arranged meeting place, trying to change Otis' mind. Otis insisted on going through with it and George lost his head, started pounding."

"You got it." Joe held the door for Tom. The blast of air conditioning hit him squarely. He liked natural heat better. "What're you ordering?"

"Usual. Burger, fries, onion rings, tall iced tea." Tom dropped his voice. "Now that's what I want me own moustache to resemble; the lad behind ye there."

The moustache Tom mentioned stepped up to the counter beside Joe. The gangly and callow young man, more a boy, sported a handsome sandy-brown brush for one so young. His thick sideburns made his face look rounder than it was. Tom had a long, long way to go.

They placed the two orders as one to save time. Joe waited until they were settled in a booth with the tray between them before he picked it up again.

"George is a possibility in our shooting, but not a probability. I don't think he was holding out on me."

"His face and hands looked as if he were leveling,

aye. Ye know, we may be right back at square one on this thing."

"Wonderful." Joe sat quiet a few minutes, chewing and sipping and thinking. "You going back to the office?"

"Aye, unless you've a better plan."

"My brain's bogging down. I could use a little peace and quiet. Drop me off at the Art Museum. I'll talk to Sommers a little, see if Schumacher said anything to him about this Burnside mess, maybe just sit on a bench in the silence and sort things out awhile. You take the car back. I'll walk down in a couple hours. It's not that far from McDowell to Washington."

The Phoenix Art Museum more than met Joe's expectations for quiet. His Wellingtons ticked like a grandfather clock through empty and echoing corridors. He climbed the curving staircase past *The Leek Seller* hung at the landing. He stopped a few moments to admire the miniature Thorne Rooms—they never failed to fascinate him—but he wouldn't give two bucks for the whole wing of modern art. Blobs. Formless shapes. Splashes. Warped and twisted, dark and baggy-eyed suffering faces . . .

Brent Sommers was not in his office.

The temporary exhibit of Southwest Indian Art, now in its third week, stood almost unvisited, a victim of the summer doldrums. Floor-to-ceiling plywood panels confined it to its own end of the second-floor el. A uniformed officer stood at its entrance. Joe knew him only casually.

"Morganstern, I believe. Stu? Lou? Rodriguez."

"Homicide, right? You were close. Hugh. Good

memory. We only met once, on that Ringgardner thing. Your partner's the Irishman."

"Tom Flaherty."

"I passed him on Robbery third floor a couple days ago. What'd he do to his lip there? Hope it ain't catching."

Joe grinned. "I can't wait to tell him, but I won't name names. How's it going?"

"What you see is what we got 99 percent of the time."

"So who wants it lively? Lively's for street cops."

"Good point."

Joe turned to a sour-looking young woman sitting at a small table between the plywood panels. An empty cash box sat open in front of her.

Joe held his badge at a comfortable angle for her. "Is Brent Sommers around?"

"I wouldn't know. Employees can enter the exhibit from either end. You would have to have a ticket to get in."

He glanced at Morganstern. The cop grinned and shrugged. No help there.

"Tell you what, Miss. I'm going back through looking for Mr. Sommers. Strictly business. I promise I won't enjoy the exhibit unless I get a ticket." He skirted the table and passed through the plywood portals.

Behind him he heard the woman's frustrated, "Officer!"

And Morganstern's cheery, "Sorry, lady, he's a sergeant. He outranks me."

The exhibit was housed in vertical glass cases, seven feet high at least, arranged in staggered fashion like a maze. You could spend three hours in here and not really see it all. Behind him a freight train roared. He turned carefully to watch as three girls in short shorts came wheeling around the far corner on skateboards. He ducked back, nearly out of view as he recognized the flouncing bush of red hair on their leader. What in heaven. . . ?

They laughed and chattered to a noisy halt in front of the table. Morganstern stepped up. "You ladies get the skateboards outta here. You're old enough you ought to know better. And carry 'em out. Don't scoot."

It figured Bernice would be their spokesman. "I looked it up in the city ordinances and tariffs. Skates are out, but the ordinance fails to mention skateboards. Sorry."

"Well, they're not going into the exhibit." The sour woman folded her arms.

"Hey, you really going in there?" The girl beside Bernice, a bleached blonde, bulged out over her faded cutoffs.

"Yeah. Why not?"

"All it is is baskets and stuff. My old lady has a whole living room full of that stuff. I'm going down to the lobby for a cigarette."

"Me too." The third girl was nearly as well endowed as Bernice.

Bernice handed the woman a little yellow ticket. "Suit yourself. Meetcha downstairs then. This won't take me long."

Joe heard Morganstern over at the wall phone. "Yeah. The rule on skateboards, chapter and verse."

Joe sure didn't need Bernice bugging him now. He stepped aside behind a case and listened as the skateboard rolled a few feet and went silent. Her rubber-soled shoes made no sound he could follow. This was an unforeseen delay. He sighed and started looking at the kachinas in front of him, killing time. Most of them resembled the monsters he heard about that dark night. So far he wasn't breaking his promise to that woman; he wasn't enjoying it.

Bernice was at the far end of the room now. "Hey, what're you doing?"

Brent Sommers' voice sounded startled, sharp. "Nothing. And get that skateboard out of here."

"You work here?"

"Yes. Go enjoy the exhibit."

"If you work here, you won't work here long. It's stupid, what you're doing. I know enough about silver to know you don't just wad a piece like that up and stuff it in your pocket. You'll bend it, break the links. Show a little respect for this stuff, huh?"

Respect? Bernice? Joe listened fascinated as he moved from case to case toward the voices.

Bernice's voice tightened, took on a frightened edge. "You don't really work here. I bet you . . ."

Joe bolted forward. Bernice came hurtling out from between cases and slammed into him.

Sommers skidded to a halt behind her with three feet to spare. He gaped, and his eyes got wide as Kansas. "Rodriguez!"

"Bingo. What's going on here?"

"Throw that young woman out. She's being abusive."

At the same time Bernice was yelling, "He's stealing some of this stuff! I saw him."

"What's in your pocket there, Sommers?"

"Show me the search warrant."

"Burglary in progress doesn't need one. Don't try to be an amateur lawyer. Turn around, please, and put both hands on your head. Lace your fingers together."

From the entrance, Morganstern called to Bernice, "Hey you! You're busted!"

Sommers lashed out wildly, clipping Bernice, pushing her against Joe. Joe saw a flash of metal and it wasn't silver. He shoved Bernice behind the nearest case; her safety came first.

"Morganstern! Down! Sommers, give it up!" Joe jogged to the far end of the case with Bernice dogging his heels. He began a cautious sneak forward.

Bernice clutched his arm. "Why are we hiding from that creep? You and that other cop are the ones with the guns."

"If I saw what I think I saw, he can blow a hole in you big enough to stuff your skateboard." He jacked his voice. "Morganstern, we're after Sommers. Burglary in progress. He's armed."

Bernice's huge liquid eyes stared at the gun in his hands. "Hey, this is for real. No game."

"No game. You stay behind me. Clear behind me." Why wasn't Morganstern throwing the alarm? Joe grabbed the skateboard and hurled it through a glass case. The burglar alarm went off museum wide. Joe could just picture the light board twinkling in the guardroom.

Two guns blasted almost simultaneously. Joe saw Sommers dive across an aisle just ahead.

"Hugh? You all right?"

"Yeah. You see him?"

Sommers dashed out, fired toward Morganstern's end and kept moving, gone again among the cases. His record didn't suggest any guerrilla duty, but he certainly knew the techniques. A moment later he popped out, fired again, and dived to safety. A glass case shattered and Morganstern fell back clutching his face.

Joe wished someone would turn off the alarm bell. Enough is enough. He started working toward the rear door.

Bernice clung so tightly she pulled him off balance. "Are you really Mexican? I mean the part that's not Indian?"

"My father's half Yaqui, half Mexican. My mother's English, immigrated from Chelsea. I was the only Chicano kid in South Phoenix Elementary who spoke English with a British accent and Spanish with a Yaqui accent." He murmured in her ear, his face only millimeters from those huge green eyes. "Lie down flat and stay there. Can I trust you to stay put?"

"Whatever you say, Sir Winston." She started to slip down, paused, kissed him a quick peck on the cheek, and plopped flat on her anything-but-flat anatomy. She even had the presence of mind to cover her head with her arms.

Sommers could be anywhere among those cases on the far side of the main aisle. Joe saw a flurry of black at the plywood—museum guards. They prudently remained at the entrance.

A tan jacket flashed by at the far end of the cases. Sommers was indeed headed for the service door at the back. Probably no guards had thought to cover that exit, since only personnel had keys to it.

Joe moved as quickly as his pounding head would let him toward that back door. He flattened against the end of a case and waited. A hand in a tan coat sleeve appeared at the door, inserted a key, twisted. The door clicked quietly, gently, moved open ever so silently. Joe waited. Waited. Waited.

Sommers bolted for the stairwell and Joe lunged. If his timing was off, he'd successfully slam a door to which he had no key and thereby help his quarry escape. But his timing was good. Sommers howled as the door clapped shut on his arm and leg. Beyond the door the gun blammed harmlessly, echoing in the steel and stucco stairwell.

Joe pressed his gun against the man's neck. "Let me hear it fall."

Metal clattered to cement beyond the door. Joe relaxed his weight against the door and gave a yank. Sommers popped backward and fell, off balance, at Joe's feet. He stayed down, his arms spread wide.

Joe heard Bernice rustle and expected her to latch onto him again, but she sprinted away down center aisle toward the entrance. She dropped down beside Morganstern and reached for his bloody face with both hands.

The danger past, Joe was instantly surrounded by solicitous museum guards in basic black. A concho belt and a squash-blossom necklace spilled partway out of Sommers' pocket. The man was promising to explain everything, but Joe snapped the cuffs on without listening. Four guards should be able to handle it now. Joe headed for Morganstern. By the time he got there, Bernice had pulled her shoes off and was using her knee-high socks to control the bleeding.

She grinned at Joe, cool as vanilla ice cream. "The glass cut him, is all. He's not hit, I don't think. Were you?"

"I don't think so." Morganstern's skin color suggested he might be about ready to throw up.

Joe squatted down beside her. "This is two I owe you."

"Good. You can start repaying by taking me out to dinner tonight. Pick me up at the house around 7."

Hot Date

Joe held the car door for her. Bernice swung her legs out, fished a key ring from her purse, and stood up. He followed her not to the winding staircase but to the cable car terminal. She groped behind a waist-high post, stabbing with the keys. From somewhere in the darkness above, the cable car groaned and began to rattle.

"I wondered how you summon that ore bucket from down here."

She giggled. "Ore bucket. Bet you visited Mine Town Amusement Park."

"When you have kids the age of mine, you've seen 'em all. You must have been there yourself, or you wouldn't know they have an operating mine shaft."

"Only once. That's where I learned I have claustrophobia." She shuddered. "Hideous place. Commercial. So hokey. Gunfight at 2 P.M. daily, for crying out loud."

"Being in a real one kinda takes the edge off playacting."

"I was so scared I wasn't scared, know what I mean? This afternoon, I mean."

He nodded. "I don't remember the technical term for it; it's not *transference. Decompensation?* Anyway, to relieve tension, your brain shifts gears temporarily. Like exploring my ancestry right in the middle of the trouble."

"Oh poop! You mean I reacted normally to something? There goes my image. Half English, huh? Ten Downing Street English. That's all right! How's your Morganstern?"

"Your diagnosis was correct—just glass cuts. He came within a sixteenth of an inch of losing an eye. Other than the fact he looks like he kissed a lawnmower, he's in good shape. They sewed him up and sent him home. Tom called his wife later. He's fine."

"Speaking of Tom and Gretchen. I did not have a double date in mind when I suggested dinner this afternoon."

The car clunked to a halt in front of them and she hopped in. He stepped in beside her and yanked the cotton cord. The bucket lurched and started its jolting climb. "I know you didn't."

"You're a stinker sometimes. In fact, you're just plain dull sometimes. I can't figure out why I had such a good time tonight. No grass, no booze, and no good music. Well, kinda good music. It should have been abysmally boring."

"Good company and the best pizza in town is a

pretty fair mix. I'm glad you weren't abysmally bored." He leaned on the back edge and watched the galactic glory of nighttime Phoenix spread out below them.

"You and Tom fit together so comfortably. You see cop shows on TV, and they fit like that, but you don't think it happens for real. For TV they work on creating the right mix. It isn't spontaneous."

"We've been together a little over four years. When I made plainclothes and transferred to homicide, they called me Don Quixote behind my back. They figured I got there by affirmative action rather than ability, and that I'd do a lot of flailing around without accomplishing much. That made Tom Sancho Panza."

"Don Quixote and Sancho Panza, huh? Do they still call you that?"

"Yeah, but once the lieutenant calculated that our conviction rate is over 95 percent, the intent changed. Now they say it to my face, and it's not malicious."

"Neat story. The circles I grew up in, there isn't any affirmative action. No Don Quixotes." She pressed in warm and close. The light-spangled view before them was no doubt old hat to her, but it seized her attention, all the same. The car clunked violently to a stop, snapping Joe's head back and making his ears ring. He gave her a hand out, and they strolled across the dark lawn. Ginia had left a night-light on in the kitchen and the light of a TV set flickered in a far upstairs room. The house was otherwise dark.

She leaned against the sliding glass door.

"Wanna come along up to my room?"

"Thanks, but no thanks. You can find your way."

"Maybe take a walk out to the garden shed, if you feel uncomfortable about going in the house." She shrugged. "It'd be interesting. Kinda kinky, among the hoes and fertilizer."

"You've been eating white bread all your life, and now you want to try out some whole wheat?"

She snickered. "Not exactly, but recreational, you know? Nothing serious. It doesn't mean that much to me anymore."

"I feel sorry for you."

"First time anyone said that. Ginia rubs her two fingers together and says, 'Naughty, naughty!' Mom doesn't say anything, but then how can she? Have you met my father?"

"No."

"That's right. Because he's hardly ever home. He's not home tonight. He gets detained here and there. It was Tucson this time. A two-hour drive and he couldn't get home. Sometime he's here, I'm gonna ask him how many ladies he has on the line. Mom says I don't dare, but I do. I dare just about anything."

"I'll buy that. So since your father's not perfect, you figure you can do anything you want? Thought you were smarter than that."

"You're so straight you make an arrow look like a garage-door spring. I can't believe you."

"I'm a darned sight more content than you are." He should be putting in a plug for Jesus here somewhere, and he had no idea how to or where to begin. Marie called him—all Christians—ambassadors for Christ. Ambassador for Christ? Hah.

Her face softened. "Cheap shot! No fair using the truth to make a point." She brightened. "Now that you've taken me home, you're going down to join Tom and Gretchen, I bet. And have some real fun."

"Tom definitely. Gretchen I don't know. But from your point of view, it'll be abysmally boring. We'll be talking shop for maybe another two hours tonight, trading information. We always tell each other everything we learn during the day. Business."

"And you can't do that when I'm around. Little pitchers have big ears. Hey, news flash. I'm not that little anymore."

"More than that. You're a suspect in a murder case."

"That's the second time you said that. You're putting me on, right?"

"Never. Wanna do me a favor?"

"Sure."

"Find me that Lawrence you used to run around with."

"That's not gonna be easy. I'll see. What do I get for it?"

"I don't know. I'll think about it."

"You do that." She arched up on tiptoe and gave him another of those coy little pecks.

Oh, why not? She was his date, after all. He wrapped around her in a proper embrace and kissed her softly. Gretchen was so right—this little pistol had gotten to him, and it sure wasn't paternal. The kiss intensified instantly and lingered far longer than he intended.

A highly sophisticated lady lurked in this flippant child body. She snuggled firmly against him, moving, pressing. She knew exactly how to excite a man. With Marie, Joe had realized how very hungry for affection he had been. Now Bernice was showing him how hungry he still was.

He forced himself to break off the kiss. He planted brief pecks on her closed eyelids, rotated her, and gave her curvaceous fanny a gentle swat to send her inside. He didn't fully realize until he was driving back down the mountain how close he came to going along up to her room.

Half an hour later he was sitting in a padded booth in Doughnut Harry's, unable to shake the memory of her kiss.

Gretchen waved an arm toward the jukebox. "The orchestra's going home. Shall we call 'em back for an encore?"

Joe flipped his only quarter across the table.

She scooped it up and two more from Tom and walked off. Tom watched her move and sighed appreciatively.

"So tell me," asked Joe, "what she thinks of your moustache-cultivating efforts there."

"Well now. I told her what every good farmer's daughter already knows: ye have to work your way through a little underbrush to reach the very best picnic grounds. She was dubious. And wait'll meself bespeaks that Hugh Morganstern! Catching. Humph."

"Did he say how he knew something was fishy?"

"That 'hey you'? Aye. He was calling Bernice, not Sommers. Skateboards be strictly forbidden, and he was going to nail her for pulling a fast one on him. He was sore put out."

"She's very good at pulling fast ones."

"Indubitably. In truth, I was a wee bit anxious for your morality there—taking the lady home. Ye got back here a lot faster 'n I anticipated ye would."

"You? Anxious about my morality?" Joe laughed. Tom's reputation as a ladies' man was a curious thing. He never mentioned conquests. Girls didn't talk about him. And yet, as did the rest of the department, Joe knew that Tommy cut a wide swath.

Gretchen slid into the booth against Tom. "You two put Sommers through the wringer this afternoon. He seems like a shaker who'd never do anything to endanger his march up the ladder of success. Why'd he do it?"

"He was truly disgusted with himself for panicking." Tom slipped his arm across Gretchen's shoulders. "Reading betwixt his words today, I ken that he realized too late 'twas only his word against Bernice's. Any little excuse—rearranging the display, making minor changes, transferring some pieces—would've worked, had he only thought of it in time."

"He claims police harassment made him panic when actually he was innocent of wrongdoing. I imagine that'll be his plea." Joe's head kept telling him he should go home to bed.

"Harassment. Sure."

"Interesting," said Tom, "that he sported a firearm of the same caliber that felled Mouse and Banks."

"Ballistics aren't done yet, but Doug's giving it

priority." Gretchen squirmed in tighter against Tom. "That's one we're all looking forward to eagerly. You still didn't say why he did it."

"As ye say, he doesn't seem the type for major larceny."

Joe's brain wasn't totally out in the woodshed. A few things at least were coming together. "How about this? He was afraid of being upstaged. I flipped through his desk calendar this afternoon. He and his wife are booked into a three-week cruise of the Inside Passage, starting the day the exhibition closes."

"So?" Gretchen shrugged. "He's glad the responsibility's out of his hair."

"Not the day *after* the exhibit is on its way. The day it goes. He helps pack up, but he doesn't get to wave good-bye because he's already in Seattle."

"Ah ha!" Tom grinned. "Pocket a few odd pieces whilst packing it up, and by the time the shortage is discovered, the stuff is elsewhere. Many other suspects handled it since he did, and he looks so innocent, enjoying a well-earned vacation. Ye said 'upstaged.' Afraid another thief might beat him to it?"

"Or cause the exhibit to close prematurely, before he could play out his plan."

"Got a better one, boys. He swipes some choice pieces now; nobody goes around daily counting the stuff; and then they turn up missing when Pete Marks' tip happens. The other thief takes all the blame, Sommers takes a few of the goodies. He probably figures he's underpaid anyway." Gretchen peered forlornly into her empty hot chocolate mug.

Tom wagged his head and dug for his wallet.

"You're a costly date, me dear. *Two* cups of hot chocolate. Would ye like another doughnut to blot it up with?"

"If you don't mind my putting on ten pounds."

He handed her a five. "Far be it from me to criticize the shape of your fanny. I'd like another bear claw whilst you're up."

"Joe?"

"Maple bar, since Tommy's buying."

She nodded and left.

Tom sprawled out across his half of the booth. "Since I'm the last of the big spenders, I'll squander a penny for your thoughts. You're pensive again. Still Bernice?"

"If Gretchen guessed right, there's a possible link between Banks and Sommers."

"Not necessarily. We don't think Sommers started filching goodies until yourself told him about the tip."

"That's true. So far, then, there's no real connection between Banks and anyone else we've talked to. We've handed Pete another plum and we're still at first base. He's going to be madder 'n hops. We spring another theft for him."

"Been meaning to speak with ye about Pete. I think I've a handle on the problem." Tom glanced toward the counter. Gretchen was giving the boy her money. "Later."

Joe watched Gretchen approach balancing a cup and three doughnuts, but his mind was far away. A connection. And Bernice. Why, out of all the madding crowd in this Valley of the Sun, was it Bernice in that hall?

Gretchen handed Tommy his change and plunked herself down. "Do your thinking out loud and we'll help you."

"Argh!" Tom snorted. "When he's thinking, he's as much fun as kinks in a garden hose. Hopeless case, he is."

"We can't be bugged, Tom."

"Ye lost me."

"How did Bernice know I was upstairs in the art museum?"

"Chance." Gretchen sipped her steaming chocolate. "She's a patroness of the arts."

"That vixen? Bullhonky." Tom bit a toe off his bear claw and talked with his mouth full. "We were talking in the Extraburger, front step of the store . . . no place to put a bug."

Bernice. That shovel coming at him. Bernice's shape in the wet shirt. Her startled voice among the display cases. Her warm body snuggled tight against him. Bernice.

Volcanoes and Canoes

This was the cheapest apartment Joe had ever been in and he saw some doozies now and then. A scarred, aged sink stood on lead-pipe legs threaded at the bottom. The only light was a naked bulb at the ceiling with a string dangling from its socket. The tiny refrigerator snored, the stove smelled of butane, and the table jiggled. Joe was half afraid the chair under him would collapse.

Robert Hask's girlfriend poured coffee with one hand and clutched at her buttonless bathrobe with the other. "I still don't know why you came here."

"Lawrence Banks listed as his number a pay phone in his apartment building. There were twenty-three other numbers penciled on the wall around the phone, and yours was one of them. So we're checking them out."

She stared at him. "They cut our phone last month."

"That's why I'm stopping by. Do either you or Bobby know Lawrence Banks? Loop?"

She sat down in a chair just as rickety as Joe's. "Yeah, we know him. Knew him, I mean. We saw him in the news. I woulda never dreamed you people were that careful. Thorough." She sipped at her coffee, watching him like a cat, suspiciously, her eyes never leaving his face.

"When's the last time you or Bobby spoke to him?"

"Not long before he, uh . . ." She seemed to be picking through words cautiously, fearfully, as if one of them might explode. "That falling-out between Bobby and Loop, that was all patched up. Mended. They were on good terms again when Loop, uh . . . you know." She pushed at her stringy blond hair.

"Can you tell me about the falling-out?"

"Wasn't that big a deal, really. Bobby went to some sort of religious meeting at Sun Devil Stadium last April. Since then he's been going to church every week, sometimes twice a week. Wednesdays. And he's got himself going straight. Loop thought he was nuts and said so. Bobby said Loop was going to hell on a greased pole. They got over it."

"Persis Magen's evangelistic meetings?"

"Yeah. Did you go to those?"

"Business. I was in on that car bomb case." *And I made a commitment like Bobby's, and I fell in love with Persis Magen's assistant. But I'm not going to mention either of those things.*

"Bobby kept asking me to go, but I don't want none of that stuff. You go off the deep end once you get started in it, you know? Like Bobby's making noises now about either we get married or he moves out."

"When did Bobby and Loop argue? Remember?"

"When was the volcano in South America?"

"Five weeks ago. Six."

"Yeah, well I told them they were like that volcano. Blowing up and messing everything up and not gaining anything by it. But you know? Bobby cried when he found out about Loop. He cried. Men are weird. Especially when they get religious. Sure you don't want some coffee?"

"Thanks, but I just came from breakfast. How'd he find out?"

"The paper. He picks up the paper and there's Loop looking at him dead."

"Bobby and Loop ever double up on jobs? Work together?"

"No. Bobby stays straight. Loop and him were friends anyway, but Bobby didn't get into stuff you can do time for."

"He at work now?"

"Yeah. He leaves at 6. I don't leave till 10:30."

"Anyone you know who worked with Loop? Other friends?"

"Loop didn't have much in the way of friends. He was nice enough, understand. I liked him okay. Bobby really liked him a lot. But Loop didn't mix it up with people much. No, I don't know anyone Loop would work with. He preferred working alone." She frowned. "Did you really get our name off the wall at the apartment house?"

"Really. Loop had an address book in his apartment, but you two weren't in it."

She wagged her head. "Loop had to have our phone number in his head, he called here so often. Before we got so far behind and they . . . you know. Maybe Bobby left a message and someone wrote it down once or something."

"Where does Bobby work?"

"Encanto Park. On the grounds. Not full time. He's an intermittent, you know? An assistant maintenance engineer and groundskeeper, I think is the title. Rakes leaves and turns on the sprinklers."

Joe thought, *And Hask's keys would fit the same locks Hawkins' did.* "And you?"

"Mother Malarkey's. I'm a waitress."

"Over on Seventh?"

She nodded.

"Do you or Bobby know a Robert Hawkins? He's a city employee also."

"Hawkins. I don't. No. Bobby might." She studied the marred tabletop in silence awhile. "Seeing Loop dead really ripped Bobby. I hope you find who did it."

"We're working on it." Joe wrote *Mighty Mouse* and *Lawrence Banks/Loop* on his card. "If you think of anything that might help us, anything at all, here's the number." He handed it to her. "Ask to speak with anyone working on the cases I jotted down there."

"Mighty Mouse?"

"The switchboard operator will know." Joe stood up. "Thank you very much, Miss Murphy. Twenty past eight—too early to drop you off at work, I guess."

She smiled for the first time. Her chair creaked as she stood up. "I get a ride with one of the other waitresses. Thanks anyway for the offer." She led the way to the door and paused with her hand on the knob. "I wish I knew something to help you. I really do. He was Bobby's friend, not mine, but I'm sorry he . . . you know."

"I know." He studied the weathered doorjamb. He yearned to say something, but somehow it didn't seem right. "I'm not speaking as a police officer now, and certainly not as a representative of the city, but as a private citizen. Understand what I'm saying? And as a private citizen, I encourage you to investigate what Bobby already knows regarding this Jesus business. He's on the right track. Go to church with him. Listen. Read. I'm afraid that when he goes to heaven, you'll be left behind, and I'd hate to see that happen. Good day, Miss Murphy."

Congratulations, Rodriguez. What you just did is probably illegal. But somehow he didn't care. He stepped from dismal gloom into cheerful morning.

The bright sun forced his eyes closed. He noticed for the first time since that shovel that his constant headache was letting up a little.

Would Marie have been proud of him? He shouldn't be doing it for Marie, but for Jesus.

Joe pulled into the Encanto Golf Course parking lot off Fifteenth Avenue, passed the sign saying "Golfers Only" and parked. At this time of year it was never full. He walked over to the park administrative office. They'd know where Bobby Hask was, probably. It hadn't opened yet. He was on his own.

He climbed the grassy knoll by the bandstand looking for workmen. No one. His right leg bound up, so he waited a few minutes for it to shake loose. He continued out under the sun to the top end of the pond and stopped.

A canoeist in a broad, floppy hat came paddling toward him, leaving a zigzag wake. If the canoe rental was open now, the office probably was. He headed down along the pond shore.

The canoeist headed straight toward him. She looked as smug as a cat in a fish cannery. "Ride, handsome?" She ran the bow up into the bank and anchored her paddle in the muck.

Joe felt himself gaping, and for many long seconds he could not gather the presence of mind to ungape. "I don't believe this. If it's all the same, Bernice, I think I'll walk. You might dump me in the drink."

"Promise I won't. Besides, I pull you out of the water, I don't throw you in. Remember?"

Against his better judgment he stepped into the bow, both hands on the gunwales, and pushed off with one foot. He'd taken the kids out in these things often enough to know a few things about staying dry. Bernice must know nothing at all about canoes, the way she flailed and splashed.

He sat backward in the bow seat so as to face her. "All right, how'd you get a handle on where I am?"

"I'm just out enjoying a little early morning boating. What are you doing?"

"And you just happened to be cruising the museum yesterday. To quote Tom, 'Bullhonky.' And I know you weren't following me. I've been watching for your Jag. So what's your source?"

"It's a small world. Where are you taking me tonight?"

"Nowhere. I'm booked. Can you point us toward the office?"

"If we were on the border, I couldn't point it toward Mexico. Here. You drive." She tossed him the paddle. "Do we have to change seats?"

"We're backward, but it's not worth the risk of tipping over to switch. When did you get here?" Sitting backward in the bow seat didn't offset him too badly. And paddling a canoe with Bernice in it was a far sight nicer than taking his kids for a boat ride. The kids kept trailing their fingers in the water, leaning over the gunwales, making the canoe list. She simply sat there and looked bounteous in a baggy gauze top.

" 'Bout ten minutes ago. You said your kids were growing up without a mother, so you're not living with anybody now. Got a girlfriend?"

"In Waukesha. She's coming out in September or October."

"Where's Waukesha?"

"Wisconsin."

"Heckuva commute. Must be 2,000 miles."

"Almost on the button."

She watched him a minute. "Your right hand there. You have it cupped over the top of the paddle but you're not holding it. When you pulled me out of the swimming pool . . . remember when you did that?"

"Vividly."

"Aren't you ashamed, now that I saved you? Anyway, you didn't grab me except with your left hand. And your foot drags sometimes. Not often."

"It's not polite to call attention to disabilities."

She smirked. "I know. So what happened? You get shot?"

"Run over. Trying to arrest a stock-car driver."

"Where was he?"

"In second gear at the time."

"I mean . . ." She paused and cackled. She sobered somewhat. "I remember that. It was in the paper. It said you'd be in a wheelchair for life. But that was a long time ago."

"Took me almost a year to get back to where I am now."

She peered beyond his shoulder. "How do you do that?"

"Do what?" He glanced behind.

"Our wake is a straight line. Keep it going straight without switching your paddle from one side to the other?"

"It's called the J stroke. Next time you're at the library, besides the sex novels and physiology texts, pick up a Boy Scout canoe manual."

"If you'll bring me here to practice."

He turned the canoe and nosed it into shore. This was as close to the office as he could get on water. She hopped out cat-quick to make way for him, holding the curved end, keeping it steady.

He crawled forward with both hands on the gunwales, hoping and sweating that he wouldn't disgrace himself in the final moments of the cruise by falling in. "Thanks for the lift, skipper. And thanks for not dumping me."

"I promised, didn't I?"

"Hey, you!" A short man in coveralls came toward them, rake in hand. "If you're gonna rent them @#$%& things, learn how to use 'em. You w—"

Joe cut him off. "Mind your language in front of the lady!" He flashed his badge, just for emphasis.

The dumpy fellow cast a sidelong glance at Bernice. "Yeah. You were sitting backward in the d— . . . the thing. Ain't no rowboat, you know."

"I'm looking for Robert Hask."

"Ain't any."

"How about Hawkins?"

"Hawkins? Me too. And if you see him before I do, you can tell him for me that he's fired."

"Why? Late today?"

"Today hell. Ain't showed up all week. That a— that Hawkins just disappeared."

Novice Gumshoe

Tom stood on the headquarters steps and straightened his tie. Beads of perspiration glistened among his rudimentary moustache hairs. "The temperature in Galway is no doubt 62 degrees and everybody's walking about in sweaters. What am I doing here, I ask meself?"

"Watering your moustache. They say anything'll grow in this climate if you just water it enough." Joe started down the steps to the cruiser parked at the red curb. "I talked for an hour to that second cousin of Banks and got nothing useful. He's not holding out, either, I don't think."

"And Harley was right about that ex-girlfriend with the tattoo. Not all her marbles roll in a straight line."

Joe reached the curb, thought a moment about what he'd just seen, and muttered, "Play along." He raised his voice. "Guess that leaves the Jones fellow out at Pueblo Grande." He patted his pockets. "Forgot my notebook with those names in it. Be right back." He glanced at the little black Mustang as he turned and jogged back up the steps. He stopped inside the glass doors to watch the car. Tom was watching it now also, surreptitiously, in the cruiser's sideview mirror.

In the black Mustang parked at the first metered space east of the red curb, a young man folded his newspaper and got out. He crossed to a row of freestanding phone booths by the bus stop, groping in his pocket for change. Joe slipped out the doors the moment the man's back was turned and jogged the length of the building. He heard the words "Pueblo Grande" as he stepped up behind the phone booth.

The boy was saying good-bye. Joe reached around and snatched the receiver from his hand. "Don't bother, Bernice. I'm not really going there after all." He hung up without listening for a response.

The boy stared, then wheeled. Tom stood behind his shoulder.

Tom pointed at his lip. "The moustache! He was right behind us at the Extraburger. I remember remarking upon his moustache."

"I noticed it when he put down the sports page and picked up the funnies. Shall we step inside and discuss this?"

"Now hold on!" The boy raised both hands. "I haven't done a solitary thing illegal, or even suspect." He looked in his early twenties.

"No one said you did. I want to find out why you're tagging me and what connection you have, if any, with the cases under investigation."

"I can tell you that much right now. None." The boy held out his hand. "Lawrence Dobbs. I'm a political science major at ASU. Clean record. Not even a traffic violation."

Joe ignored the handshake offer. "No doubt. Poly scis all play cops and robbers on the side."

"That's it exactly. My career goal is CIA. Barring that, a private investigator. Since I'm not licensed yet, I offered Bernice a tail on you, just for the practice. Great practice, right? I mean, you're a professional."

"Right. That must be why I caught on to you in only three or four days. Inside."

Lawrence Dobbs shrugged and walked inside. They worked on him almost two hours. He was still Bernice's boyfriend, but among his many pre-career exercises he was practicing going undercover. Thus it seemed to Ginia he was no longer coming around the Thompsons. He had, in fact, been at the same pool party Tom and Joe attended—the tram operator, his sandy-blond hair and moustache rinsed dark. And he had no connection, however remote, to Banks, to silver, or to thefts, except in his relationship with Bernice. They sent him home with instructions to tail someone else for practice.

By now it was pushing 5 o'clock. Joe leaned on the main desk—he still got dizzy when he moved quickly—as Benny argued politely with the holder of a parking ticket.

Tom leaned beside him. "Let's take tomorrow off. We've worked straight through the weekend. I'll snatch Gretchen away from her clammy and uninviting lab. Take her out for lunch and a drink. The TV log claims *Casablanca's* on tomorrow."

"Oh, I see. 'Taking out to lunch' means your place."

He grinned. "Cold cuts and good Irish whiskey. Ye can't do better. Ye might well do the same—take the day off, I mean."

"I could take the kids over to that new water slide in Tempe." Joe stood erect, waited until his ears quit ringing, and started out the door. "We'd better take Rocinante. We'll want to bring him in if he's there."

"Got the keys right here." Tom jingled them.

That new little file clerk from Records was just coming in. She grabbed Tom's arm and brought him to a stop. "Hey, what's this? Not bad, Irish. Very cultural."

"Eh? Ah. Me moustache."

She studied his lip closely. "There's a lot of different styles, you know. Handlebar. Fu Manchu. David Niven Pencil. This one's a Stonehenge, right?"

"Stonehenge?" Tom's brows crowded together.

"Sure, you know. A little something sticking up here, a little something sticking up over there . . . G'bye, Irish." She trotted away giggling.

"Disgusting damsel." Tom stomped out the door to the cruiser mumbling all the way.

The cruiser named Rocinante should have been red-lined years ago. The right door latch poised on the brink of total disintegration. The engine was shot, the upholstery worn. The front seat was especially battered, for Joe had this habit of scrunching down in the corner, draping his left arm the length of the seat back, and bringing his left knee up to chin level. A permanent heel mark dented the seat there.

Joe curled up in his corner now and left the driving to Tom. The puzzle had pieces missing—important pieces—but the odd pieces fit none of the holes. It was as if they were assembling two or three different jigsaw puzzles from a common pile of pieces.

Robert Hask was not home, nor did they really expect him to be. They drove on over to Mother Malarkey's.

Tom parked facing the patio with its red plastic tables and chairs. From here they could watch Carol Murphy working inside. "She gave ye no inkling at all that the lad had flown the coop?"

"Not a glimmer. It's as if she didn't notice he was gone."

"Ye realize, I trust, that after all this work, we're not yet to first base."

"We haven't left the plate. What if it was a contract job?"

"Argh. I was discounting the prospect of a professional hit because of the gunman's sorry angle. A true pro would surely pick a better spot."

"Can't fault the effectiveness of the place he chose."

"Aye, nor its efficiency." Tom stiffened. "She just headed for the back, and reaching for her apron strings. She's coming."

Moments later Carol Murphy pushed out the employees' door into the burning sun, stood a moment on the hot cement, and stepped down off the curb.

Joe swung out wide and walked toward her.

"Miss Murphy?"

She stopped cold, half turned, looked at Tom and heaved a resigned sigh. "I don't know anything I didn't tell you this morning."

"Carol Murphy, my partner, Tom Flaherty. You knew Bobby's been gone nearly a week, but you didn't mention it."

She chewed her lip. "That's because he's coming back any time. He's probably there right now."

"We stopped by. Not yet. Let's sit at an outside table here and talk about this."

"I don't want my boss to see me talking to cops. How it looks—you know."

"Ah! Perfect excuse to loosen me tie!" Tom clawed at his throat. "There. Incognito." He plunked down on a scorching fiberglass seat under an umbrella.

"Only cops wear sport coats in this weather." She sat.

Joe sat watching her. Tom sat watching her. She sat watching the shiny red table top. When the silence got too heavy to carry, she spoke. "Bobby took off right after Loop got killed. He said he'd be back when he got his head together. About Loop and about us. He was real shook up and confused."

"Any hints about where?"

"He likes trees and stuff. White Mountains. Flag. Oak Creek. I don't know."

Joe put a sharp edge on his voice. "He do this often?"

"Couple times before."

"How long was he gone then?"

"Couple days. Three or four days. Till his grass

ran out. But he's not using it anymore. Grass or anything. Nothing."

"What about his job? What arrangements does he make with his supervisor when he goes off like this?"

"He just takes off. He doesn't like this job anyway. Says his boss has a foul mouth. He's real big on that now. Doesn't like to be around people who swear."

"Neither do I. Does he have any other income?"

"No."

"Relatives? Friends he'd go to for help or shelter?"

She shook her head.

Tom chimed in. "Does he ever do any odd jobs for John Berendsi?"

"Who?"

"Pawnbroker and furniture store near Osborn."

"Oh, him. Odd jobs? You mean steal things? No. Bobby stays straight. I don't think he's ever even been fingerprinted."

"Anything at all, lass. Legitimate, illegal, anything."

"No." She looked at Joe. "That's something else they argued about. Loop kept selling to that pawnbroker and getting ripped off. Bobby couldn't understand why Loop didn't take his stuff somewhere else. At least some of the stuff."

"Which part of your typical haul?"

"Jewelry and guns. Berendsi won't handle TVs and microwaves."

"Where else might he sell jewelry and guns?"

She sat silent.

Tom squirmed. "The food here all right? I never tried this Mother Malarkey's, despite the lovely name of it."

"Yeah, it's all right. Too expensive even with my discount. I eat at home."

Tom stood up. "Then I'll get meself a bite. Joe?"

"Whatever looks good."

Tom trotted off.

"Does this mean you don't need me anymore?"

Joe smiled. "Naw. It means that Irishman can't stand to be anywhere near food without eating. It's near dinnertime, and it gnaws on him. Listen, Carol. Bobby's clean. You said so. Loop's dead. That means there's no one you have to protect. It doesn't matter anymore. Where else might Loop have sold jewelry?"

"Keno's. Not the big one. The little one out by Peoria. And a man named DeMuro. I forget where they find him. And the museum."

"Which museum? There are many."

"The one with all the Indian stuff—you know?"

"Heldt?"

"I guess so. Near Central, downtown."

"Who's the contact at the museum? The fence?"

"The director, I'm pretty sure." She twisted her mouth, trying to wring out the words. "I can't remember any names."

"Assistant director. Burnside? Otis Burnside?"

"No, that's not it. Besides, I remember Loop talking about it once. I'm sure the person he was talking about was a woman. Yes. The one at the museum who buys that stuff—the director—was a woman."

Hustler at the Heldt

The Heldt Museum of Indian Arts and Antiquities contained as much Yaqui material as any other collection in the world; still, that was precious little. Its classic Pima and Papago basketry was the best, its Yuma and Gila artifacts outstanding, its Apache wing carefully and correctly divided out by tribe. And its rest rooms were clean, the toilet paper soft and user-friendly. Well-rounded institution.

Joe paused in the main entry arch just off the street. Before him, three dozen big terra-cotta pots hung from the classic Spanish arches that rimmed the central patio. Dark red geraniums with bright foliage graced the pots, and some plants with delicate leaves and tiny, deep, dark-blue flowers tumbled out over the rims, softening both shape and color. George was a genius in his chosen profession.

The entrance to the museum proper was two huge, ornately carved Spanish doors at the far end of the central patio. At this end of the patio, Joe turned left, into the director's outer office.

The receptionist glanced up and glowered. "Oh, you."

Joe felt as welcome as a terrier at a cat show. "I called fifteen minutes ago."

"I remember." He punched a button and put the phone to his ear. "Detective Rodriguez." He stared past Joe. "Yes, ma'am." He hung up. "She's tied up for another ten minutes, with apologies."

"I'll wander around and be back in ten minutes." Joe left the air-conditioned chill for the warmth of the patio. On his stroll to the far end, he paused to admire those deep blue flowers up close. He pushed through the heavy carved doors and turned right, then left into the kachina room. When he visited here with the kids, they hurried him through to "more interesting" displays. Today he could look and study at leisure. No, not today. A familiar red head grabbed his attention.

Joe walked over beside the hair to gaze at some mudheads in a glass case. "Now that one, they say, looks like my Uncle Hector, but most of the family resemblances are over there in that corner."

Tom snapped around to stare at him. "And here I thought ye were taking the day off."

"And I thought you were too. Date fall through?"

"Aye. Gretchen had to go to a stabbing. Half of Maynard's techs are on vacation. But you've no excuse."

"I took the kids out to that water slide and was

back by noon. I couldn't wait to work on Dr. Schumacher a little. I want to know what happened out beyond Bapchule with Sommers, and I want to know why she deals in hot silver, and a bunch of other questions."

"I was thinking of stopping by her office meself, but when I arrived, so did some sort of salesman. When I finish here. . . ."

"Just what are you doing here?"

"I realized all our threads keep bringing us back here, and I'm not familiar with the place. So I thought mayhap I'd case the joint. See what's where and what's what."

"Stepping on Pete's toes again?"

Tom frowned. "I'm wondering if there be anything at all for Pete in this. What if the Burnside thing is what Banks heard about? The boy might've picked up a false rumor. Perhaps, even, he was selling fake info for a fast buck."

"Then why waste two people?"

"Mistaken identity? Some other matter entirely? A nut with a libido-based hatred of short women? The world's a shambles, me lad, and this case just isn't happening."

A class of schoolchildren came pouring through the door in double file. With the aplomb of a drill sergeant, their teacher barked, "Halt. We'll spend five minutes here. No one leave the room, but you can spread out and look at everything." The double line dismembered itself instantly and spattered against the glass cases.

"Meself shall go check out the remainder of this place." Tom gave Joe a nod and waded through small people to the far door. Joe smiled. Fatherhood, if it ever came to Tom, would require much adjustment.

Joe ambled back across the patio to the director's office. He hadn't given them the whole ten minutes, but it was close enough.

A matronly lady got there five steps ahead of him. Her arms were covered nearly to the elbows with silver bracelets, and she wore not one necklace but three. Joe held the door for her. She barely noticed him.

Vale Schumacher stood by her receptionist's desk shaking hands with a severe-looking young woman with a briefcase and tweed blazer. The receptionist looked buried. The tweed blazer exited, smiling.

"So sorry to just drop in," the matron crowed. "Just a moment of your time, if I may. You may not remember me, but . . ."

"Of course I do. Mrs. Wilton. One of our life members."

The matron glowed. "You employ several Indians here."

"We do." Schumacher tilted her head slightly.

"Well, I asked one of them where the nearest powder room was; that one by the Navajo hogan, you know, is out of order. And he was marvelously polite. And helpful too. He complimented several of my pieces here very knowledgeably. He makes a fine impression and is a credit to the museum. I just wanted you to know."

Schumacher opened her mouth, but the receptionist cut in. "Bob and Cherry are supposed to be off today. Are you certain it was an Indian employee?"

"Oh, yes. Unmistakably. Older man, stocky. He was wearing the tan museum uniform and carrying a huge toolbox. Upstairs in . . ."

The receptionist looked past her to Joe. "We haven't issued a jumpsuit uniform in ten years, and there are no repairs scheduled for . . ."

Joe bolted out the door and raced the length of the patio. He pushed through the double doors and on around the corner through the kachina room. He almost knocked over a little girl in a frilly dress. He yanked open the far door.

Behind him an irritated child's voice snarled, "Watch it, mister!"

And the teacher's voice, "Charles!"

He took the curving stairway to the interior lobby three steps at a time. He needed Tom now. The hall was empty. Should he shortcut through the hogan exhibit or take the main way to the silver room? He shortcutted. As he entered the Navajo wing from the south end, he saw a tan jumpsuit disappearing out a door at the north end. He covered Navajo history in three seconds and burst out through the far door. The fellow was nearly at the end of the hall already, his toolbox tucked under his arm.

"You! Stop right there! Police!"

The man glanced back and broke into a run. He was remarkably swift for being so short-legged. He disappeared into PREHISTORIC CULTURES: SINAGUAS. Joe dived right in behind him. When they passed a bewildered black couple, Joe was less than twenty feet back.

The man could descend a curving staircase as fast as Joe could. Joe thought briefly of pulling a gun and ruled against it—not with a roomful of preschoolers and who knew how many others around. Children pop up unexpectedly. The man barged into the kachina room amid squeals and gasps. Joe was close enough to have him now in moments.

The runner lurched sideways and slammed into a teacher. Knocked off balance, she collided with Joe. Together they tipped against a free-standing case. It rocked and crashed to the floor. The burglar alarm went off. Bells—piercing, jangling bells—filled the air from here to Christmas. Joe twisted free with difficulty; his headache and dizziness were interfering with both balance and vision. He plunged out the door completely winded. What must that Indian feel like?

Halfway down the patio the Indian was no longer running. He scurried, almost staggering, clutching his toolbox. Still he was fast enough that he would reach the street before Joe could reach him.

Joe might be at the end of his first wind, but Tom was fresh. He appeared from nowhere at Joe's right, already at a dead run. He headed straight for the tan jumpsuit, angling across the patio. Hot dog! Cavalry to the rescue.

Tom was almost within grabbing distance. The Indian reached out suddenly and gave one of those hanging pots a shove as he passed. It swung in a short, fast arc behind him and collided with Tom. Tom's head and shoulders stopped cold; his churning legs kept going and he splacked flat on his back on the patio bricks.

Joe quelled his impulse to stop, jumped Tom and

kept running out the big arched entryway. He noticed—a remarkably abstract observation—that his gun was in his hand now. The Indian reached the curb near the museum loading ramp. He was heaving the toolbox into the back of a battered green pickup. He flung himself into the truck bed beside the box as the driver gunned the motor and peeled out. Joe ran faster, one final, breathless burst of speed to catch a glimpse of the license plate.

The burglar alarm quit, leaving sudden, ringing silence. Panting like a spent racehorse, Joe jogged the half block back to the front entrance. As he entered the arch, Schumacher was charging from her outer sanctum to the inner one, leaving doors gaping wide open. Cold air came tumbling out to cool Joe's sweaty face.

The receptionist was waving arms. "I tried to call the police . . ."

"Good!" she shot over her shoulder.

Tom sat at Schumacher's desk with her telephone receiver at his ear. "Eh, Sammie, Tommy. Pete Marks, quick. Huh? Terrible." He cradled his head in both hands and let the receiver slide down to dangle from his fingertips.

The receptionist was still waving around behind Joe. "It is *not* good! The lines were busy and I couldn't get through. They put me on *hold!!*"

Joe reached across the desk and tipped Tom's face aside for a better look. Tom's cheek beside his right ear was already turning interesting colors. Joe grimaced. "And the final score, folks: Flowerpot, one; fighting Irish, zero. Goose egg."

"C'mon, Peter, answer it," Tom muttered.

Schumacher was fishing around in what looked like a two-foot-high refrigerator. Her rummaging produced an ice cube tray. She whanged it against a file cabinet. Tom winced. She wrapped some ice cubes in a paper towel and commenced breaking them up with a fist-sized quartz specimen from the windowsill.

Tom raised the receiver. "Pete, your biggie just popped. Heldt Museum. Talk to Joe here." He passed the phone across and accepted Schumacher's makeshift ice pack.

"Pete? All Points on a dark-green pickup vintage '60 to '64, license Arizona 844 LRQ. Dented right rear fender, no back bumper."

Pete's throaty snarl scorched the wire. "Two of homicide's finest and you watched him walk away."

"Hopi Indian; stocky; five eight or nine; probably just came from a kiva ceremony; somewhere between forty and fifty, on the fifty side. Runs like the very devil." *Or a Yaqui protective monster.*

Pete garbled something ominous sounding and broke the connection with a slam.

Tom leaned back and adjusted his ice pack. "Sure'n I shoulda stayed home. *Casablanca* too. Now how do ye figure a kiva ceremony?"

"Smelled smoke. He's permeated with it and that's the logical explanation. Dr. Schumacher, shall we go see what he did?"

"I already ordered the room roped off."

Joe glanced down at Tom. "Up to it?"

"Right with ye." Tom lurched to his feet and took a few experimental steps.

Schumacher was already hard-stepping out the door and across the patio. Joe hung back for Tommy; the Irishman wasn't moving very quickly. Joe could certainly relate to that feeling. As they pushed in through the big carved doors, a police siren howled out on the street. The receptionist would direct the troops up.

The children were lined up again double file at the far end of the kachina room. Beyond, through the opened door, Joe saw Schumacher disappearing up the inside staircase.

Behind him a child's voice asked, "What happened to your face?"

The teacher's voice warned, "Charles . . ."

And Tom replied, "Kissed a flowerpot, lad."

Upstairs, Schumacher was standing impatiently outside a roped-off side room devoted to craftsmanship in silver. A timid-looking rent-a-cop, a gray-haired older gentleman with droopy jowls, stood beside her by the posts and velvet rope. He looked immensely relieved to see Joe and Tom. He tipped a post aside for them.

The room was lined floor to ceiling with glass cases on all four sides. Exquisite examples of silversmithing adorned every square foot of case space, all artfully arranged on black velvet draperies. Joe surveyed the ton of work that had been left behind and began to understand a little better the scope of Burnside's disastrous scam. They were talking about fortune upon fortune in silver.

The cases lettered CONTEMPORARY NAVAJO and CONTEMPORARY HOPI stood open. Large patches of draped velvet were empty. But the patches were not uniform, nor were they all in easy reach of a thief snatching at random.

Tom asked, "Dr. Schumacher, have ye any clear idea exactly what was taken from here?"

"You're well aware our accession cards are in disarray. No."

Joe whistled softly and wiggled a finger at the rent-a-cop outside the door. The gentleman obediently stepped inside.

Joe smiled to warm things up. "You spend long hours in this one area; surely you've examined the displays in this room in some detail."

Schumacher cooled things off instantly. "Where were you when all this was going on?"

"At the other end of my beat, madam, in the hogan room. He must have been familiar with my circuit. He had no more than two minutes alone at this end of the hall. I never saw him."

"The silver in here." Joe pointed. "You're familiar with what was here?"

"Yes. I couldn't describe it in detail, but I know what was here pretty much. You look at it a lot when you're in one hall for eight hours."

"I was hoping so. The thief seemed to be selective. He didn't just grab whatever was handy. Up there, for example." Joe pointed. "Can you see a pattern to what he took?"

The guard studied the holes, the silver, the holes. He scratched his chin. "Understand, I'm not certain. He was kind of selective. I'd say he took a lot more Hopi stuff than Navajo. But he was nonselective in another way. Some of the Hopi work he took was worth less than some of the Navajo stuff that's still here." The man turned to hold Joe's eye. "That doesn't make sense. If he doesn't know silver, why not just grab what's easy to reach? And if he does know silver, why not take the most valuable?"

"Good point." Joe gave him another smile, another splash of warmth. The fellow was scared spitless. Joe pondered it a moment. *Why would the thief be selective in that way? Why not the costliest?*

Tom grunted. "That toolbox must've been f'looting heavy. He was limited in how much he could take by the sheer weight of it."

"And the size of the toolbox." Joe studied the case frames. "No tools used, no marks. He had keys to both the alarm system and to the cases themselves. An employee, Mrs. Schumacher."

"It would seem so, but our employment records will show you he is not. Bob and Cherry don't look anything like him."

"And how would ye know what he looks like, Dr. Schumacher?"

"Detective Rodriguez described him in my presence moments ago. The description doesn't fit." She glared at Tom. "And now excuse me. I'll try to get a list of the stolen pieces. It'll take awhile." She marched out as she had marched in—irate.

"We thank ye for your insight here, sir." Tom laid a hand on the guard's shoulder. "We'll need your statement, of course; anything ye may have thought suspicious, people approaching the description of our perpetrator. And mayhap, after all this settles down, I can talk to ye alone a few minutes."

"Of course. Look, I . . ." The old man spread his hands helplessly.

Joe fell in beside the man and started for the door. "We're taking some heat ourselves for letting him slip out from under us. Try to look at it philosophically. It'll pass."

Two uniformed officers appeared at the rope. Joe smiled at them as he swung his leg over the barrier. "Hi, Tillis. Jim. Who won yesterday?"

"The softball game? Don't ask."

"By that much, eh?" Tom pushed a post aside and squeezed by.

"Hey, what's this?" Tillis was in no position to see Tom's brand-new knot, but he was staring at his upper lip. "How long you been working on it?"

"Fortnight."

"Well, if I were you, Flaherty, I'd plow the whole crop under and replant in alfalfa." Tillis sniggered as he turned away to the silver room.

"A world full of clowns and he fancies himself funny," Tom sniffed.

They walked slowly down the hall. As they stepped out onto the landing, the school children came trooping up the curved staircase, so Tom and Joe moved aside to let them pass.

"A *flowerpot?*"

"Charles!"

The parade disappeared into the hogan exhibit.

Tom leaned both elbows on the balustrade. "Ye know, Joe? Meself was once a Charles."

Joe leaned beside him. "I don't doubt it a bit."

Psyching Pete

A desert sunset is a beautiful thing, if you're in a position to see one. Tonight, the sun was slipping to oblivion for another twelve hours and Joe was in no mood to watch it go. He was tired. His head pounded. Tommy's must feel worse; the normally ebullient Irishman had numbed out. He had ceased interviewing anyone and now sat out in the back parking lot in the command van, orchestrating telephone and radio chatter.

Not that he was needed anymore. For hours cops had been swarming all over the museum. Now they were departing by twos and threes and vanloads. The excitement was past, the day over. Sufficient unto the day is the evil thereof.

Joe's notebook had no more empty pages in it. Time to quit. He strolled out the employees' exit toward the curb. A viselike grip yanked him to a stop.

He wheeled and managed to pull his punch just in time. It was Pete. An uneasy twinge put a knot in his stomach. Pete Marks, two inches taller and forty pounds heavier, looked dark and furious enough to make the devil himself uneasy.

"Got business with you, Rodriguez."

"What can I do for you?" Joe kept his voice low and even.

"Sticking your greasy nose in is one thing. Lousing it up is something else. You were supposed to come to me when you got wind of this. To *me!* That was Mouse's killer you let walk away."

"Pete, we didn't know it was coming. We—"

"I'm busting you clear down to Talking Car and when your lieutenant gets back you're dead. Out. You won't blow anym—" His eyes bulged wide as a lanky arm clamped around his neck.

With a practiced twist Tom pulled Pete backward off balance and sat him unceremoniously on a steel junction box—a telephone or air conditioning manifold of some sort. The metal thudded under the weight. Joe latched onto Pete's other side and they both squeezed in on him.

Tom murmured in his ear, "Ye can listen to me spiel in this inelegant position, or ye can promise to sit still and hear me out. Either way, listen ye will, all the same. What'll it be?"

The arm Joe gripped relaxed a bit. Tom nodded and straightened. "Joe and I are here by chance. We each came independently to work on Schumacher a bit. We had no inkling of what was coming, and we're investigating Mouse's murder. That's what the review board'll hear, should it come to that. Now ye know what you're up against if ye care to press the issue."

He raised a hand as Pete started fussing. "I'm not done. Hear me out, for 'tis important. Meself has done some guessing and I want to know how close I've come. Picture this: Mouse is the pride of your department and you're her mentor. But when she goes down, the first man she thinks to call is Joe here. Why, that would try the patience of a saint, and a saint ye ain't. Ye feel a twinge of jealousy. Why Rodriguez, of all people?

"Then a few short hours later ye step into the abandoned room from whence Mouse's killer did his dirty work and here's Gretchen Wiemer in Joe's arms. And the body not even cold yet. Did he care nought for Mouse at all?

"And now, everywhere ye turn, these two clowns from outside your department keep anticipating ye. Popping robberies that are properly your own province. How am I doing so far?"

"You're done. And so's he." Pete started to rise.

Joe helped Tom sit him down again.

Tom cooed on in a voice to soothe raging bulls. "Back to the beginning. Mouse didn't call Joe, Pete. She asked for you. I called Lee and confirmed that. Ye see, the hospital tried to reach ye but ye were out of the office. Lee Asimoto handled Mouse in emergency, and Lee and Joe are good friends. Their kids go to the same school, same teacher, PTA buddies. So Lee called Joe because he lives less than five minutes from the hospital, and Lee knew there was no time to waste. It was Asimoto's call, not Mouse's. Ye ken?"

Black, glowering silence.

Tom continued on his roll, smooth as spun silk. " 'Tis logical that if Mouse had summoned Joe to her bedside (which as I just pointed out she did not), they must be more than just friends. Yet a few short hours later Joe and Gretchen seem much too close. Now I remind ye that no one knows Joe better'n meself, and I meself am getting to know Gretchen quite well. I can guarantee ye, Pete, there was nothing between Joe and Mouse then and there be nothing between Joe and Gretchen now. Meself pleads the fifth, but Joe is clear."

Tom held up his hand again. "One more thing. We keep bumping into your bailiwick because our cases be one and the same."

"Not *all* that."

"Yes, all that," Joe cut in. "Pete, I'm not going to say we want Mouse's killer as much as you do, because that can't be true, but we want him. Maybe it is this Hopi. But maybe not. And if it's not, we're not going to catch him by squabbling in front of a review panel. I need your help and you need me. We have to put the fighting aside until this is over and we've nailed the SOB."

Pete ripped himself to standing and glared down with fury unabated. "I said you're gone, Rodriguez, and you're gone." He stormed off.

Joe rubbed his face and his burning eyes. "You pegged it right on, Tommy, but I don't think he was listening."

"Yeah, he was." Purley Petersen stepped out of the employees' back door. "I detoured a couple cops; didn't want you three interrupted." Purley grinned suddenly.

"And listened whilst ye were at it." Tom stood up slowly, stiffly.

"Show me a good detective and I'll show you a good eavesdropper. It takes Pete awhile to digest stuff like that. Give him a couple days."

"In the meantime he pulls me a suspension." Joe felt every bit as stiff as Tom looked. "Or ousts me. My job security is iffy anyway. I don't need this. Not now."

"We'll consider options over a beer, eh?" Tommy smiled, but his lips were tight and grim.

Purley cleared his throat and read from his notebook. "The getaway truck was abandoned twice; once six years ago and again this afternoon four blocks from here. No usable prints, no identifying evidence, but the lab's still working on it. Expired plates. Once owned by a Hopi nowhere near your description who now works here in Phoenix in construction. Former owner's clean. Stan Tartoff musta worked on him for two hours."

"Abandoned on the reservation?"

"No hint where." Purley flapped his notebook shut. "I approached Pete with the idea of sending word up north, but he's convinced the perp's down here in Phoenix. The tip was here, the heist was here, the truck was here. The killings were here. He doesn't buy your kiva theory."

Maynard Rust's van rolled to the curb and Gretchen climbed out with a fistful of computer paper, her blond hair still bouncy and pert. The three of them joined her at the curb.

"Hi. I'm Snow White. These must be those two dwarfs, Bumpy and Lumpy."

Tom reached out and tickled her ear. "And what makes ye so sarcastic this evening?"

"Having to work all day. I've been a Bogart fan for twenty years. Here's Maynard's latest efforts as a ballistics expert. Sommers' gun was not *the* gun." She handed Tom the readout. "Hey, is that offer for lunch still on?"

"No, me dear, you're too late. Now the offer's for dinner." He leafed through it. "Look at this! How can a few itty pieces of lead generate all this paperwork? Nothing solid. Negatives."

"I'm sick of negatives." Joe watched for a moment the pink and orange of the sky beyond the palm trees and power lines and rooftops. He turned to Tom. "Let's do something positive once."

"Ah! Here's where ye reveal the fruit of your cogitations. You've fingered the culprit."

"Don't I wish. This case is so scattered. Tangled. So let's sort it out by suspects. Take a good hard look at our suspects one by one, put together what we know, either pin it on number one or go on to number two."

"So you don't think the Indian's our man?" Purley frowned.

"The Indian's definitely Pete's man, but I'm not so sure he's ours. Just a feeling. It's a long way from burglary to murder in cold blood, and he's active in his village's religious life. I don't have a radio or phone in my car. As long as I stay out of the office, news of any interdivisional action Pete takes can't reach me. Tommy, how about picking up a search warrant for Berendsi's and meeting there early tomorrow morning?"

"I'm for that. Meself would choose him as our favorite murder candidate. He threatened Banks, fences silver, has the right consonants in his name plus the right attitude and no alibi, and he's the right height. A weapon would improve the picture immensely, and he's got a store full of 'em."

Purley wagged his head. "Pete already had Linc and some uniforms out there checking for stolen silver, and they're staking the place out overnight, just in case there's visitors."

"That's Robbery, but did they check guns? Right after the killings we went through his inventory for a murder weapon and found nothing. He's probably not expecting us to do it again."

Gretchen dropped to one knee in front of Joe and clasped her hands together. "Oh please, kind sir, let me go along tomorrow morning. I realize it's not seemly of a post-feminist to grovel, but I do so want to see some real action. No more lab work and paper shuffling."

"What's it worth to you?"

She stood up. "Ah. Dickering means 'yes.' Dinner at that new steak house out at Cave Creek."

"You're on. Coming, Purl?"

"Ain't allowed. You're investigating murder, at least while you still got your badge. I can only investigate robbery, but then if I'm doing that you ain't allowed. I got my orders."

"So you and Gretch search the premises for stolen silver while Tom and I look for the murder weapon. We can try not to bump into each other. Say, 7 A.M.?"

The burly Purley grinned. "Never did like that

gunner. I'll be there."

Tom poked Gretchen affectionately. "Dinner-time."

Glowing like Christmas, she ran off to send the van on its way without her.

For the first time since that shovel, Joe was starting to feel good. Stiff and weary as he was, his headache was finally dissipating. He no longer felt so out of it, so abstracted from the mainstream of things. They might not be to first base yet, but he could feel a shift in the winds of chance—they were definitely leaving the plate at last.

Bobby Hask

Joe pounded on the door again. Lawrence Banks had climbed these very stairs the night before he died. The rusted iron was as dismal and in need of paint as the rest of Berendsi's premises. They crawled up the back wall of his store and ended in a rickety landing by the apartment door. Someone, in a feeble attempt at decor, had put a redwood pot out on the corner of this landing, but whatever was in it had long since died. Joe was no good at identifying brown sticks.

"We closed!" Lu Ella's sleepy voice.

" 'Tis meself, Lu Ella, Tom Flaherty. Open, please."

A door chain rattled, a deadbolt ticked. The door crept open a hair.

"Might we bespeak your John Berendsi, please?"

"He ain't here. Left 'fore I was awake."

"You're still not awake, I aver. May we come in?"

"Not suppose to let you."

Tom held the warrant up to the door. "This might help, eh?"

"One of them again?" She swung the door open. "John gonna be breathing fire when he finds out."

"Where is he?"

"Don' know. Car gone?"

"That station wagon? Aye." Tom stepped inside and Joe followed closely behind. Tom checked the bathroom as Joe wandered through the bedroom. The tiny closet, crammed with junk as well as clothes, was too small to hide a man, but he looked anyway. If they had to find something the size of a handgun in this mess, it was going to take them the rest of the fiscal year, even with a metal detector.

"Miss Parkins, does John keep a gun upstairs here?"

"Under the mattress on his side there. Other side."

Joe groped briefly, took a quick look at the stubby little 9mm and stuffed it back between mattress and spring.

"Whatcha do to your face there? Looks terrible." Lu Ella was finally starting to sound half awake.

"Eh, 'tis a long story concerning a flowerpot designed and installed by a fellow who swings shovels." Tom glanced wickedly at Joe. "Tangled web of circumstance."

"Huh?"

"Let's look downstairs first." Joe waved a hand toward the inside stairs. "Miss Parkins, would you open the front door for two other officers, please? Thank you."

She studied the search warrant. "You sure this is real?"

"Stake me badge on it. After you, Lu Ella." Tom cast one last look around the mess, wagged his head at Joe in disbelief, and followed her down the dark, creaky stairwell.

As Gretchen and Purley came eagerly through the door, Joe scanned the display case beside the register. "We want to see his pawn, Miss Parkins; the guns that aren't here."

It took her a few minutes to find the combination, to open the safe in the back office, to locate the right cardboard wine carton. Tom plunked it on Berendsi's cluttered desk. One by one he laid the guns out until the carton stood empty.

"Pawn records?" Joe looked at Lu Ella.

She handed him a battered green tin file box full of 3x5s.

Tom smirked. "Not unlike one of Schumacher's two filing systems."

Joe thumbed through the cards behind the GUNS index. "Smith and Wesson something or other; can't read the writing. Keyed to tag number 45."

"Here." Tom hefted the gun and laid it back in the box.

"Colt .38 Police Special, tag 14."

"Aye."

"Luger . . . I can't tell. Guess it's a model number. Tag 70."

"Nothing of the sort here."

Joe held the card aside. "Smith and Wesson modified, 8-inch barrel and walnut grips; 68. Colt antique, whatever that means, 63. Webley .380, pearl grips, 24. Something 9 millimeter, 97. The rest are rifles and shotguns."

"All accounted for save the Luger."

Joe tossed the card onto the desk. "He has it with him."

Tom wheeled on Lu Ella. "Ye didn't tell us he took a gun."

"I didn' know, honest! He left already." She was so frightened she squeaked.

"You know, lass, you're within an ace of being charged as an accessory. Especially if John hurts anyone with that gun."

Lu Ella looked near tears. "Them two people—Loop and the white chick—was it that kind of gun?"

Joe would have been noncommittal. Tom nodded. "Aye."

"I'm scared."

"Ye think he might use the gun on yourself?"

She heaved her shoulders—more violent and more hopeless than a mere shrug.

"Ye think he might've used it already?"

She nodded. "He was terrible teed off at Loop. Loop was high again and John can't stand nobody being high. Specially nobody with a beard. And he was afraid."

"John was afraid of Loop?"

"Afraid he'd . . . what John said was 'queer the deal.' Mess up a big job for a few bucks, he said."

"With whom was John dealing to get this windfall? Who was scheduled to do the job and bring the goodies?"

"I don' know . . ."

"He mentioned a name, surely, just in passing. A name."

The tears welled up and over. "Thass why I'm so scairt. You think I'm holding back. You gonna think I'm part of somethin' real bad. I ain't!"

Joe chimed in. "He talk about any Indians lately? Mention anything about Indians or a specific Indian?"

"Some old man on a reservation once. Thass the only Indian he ever mentioned, 'cept you. He don' know if you're Indian or Mex or what, he says. Couple weeks ago that was. About the old man. Not lately."

"No names?"

She shook her head and wiped her glassy cheeks. "You gonna 'rest me?"

"Not yet, lass. We'll be letting ye know." Tom patted her shoulder. "Leave the safe ajar for Purley and Gretch, aye? There's a good girl." He fell in behind Joe and they headed for the front door. He followed Joe out into the bright morning sun. "Let me anticipate ye; we're taking a scenic drive out to the Hopi mesas. Taking the Suburban?"

"The Midget. Since I probably won't get reimbursed for the mileage, I don't want to drive the 'Burb that distance. Pete's not sending anyone Both of us or just me. You tend to get overheated and turn violent shades of red, driving around in the desert in the middle of summer."

"Meself has a few urgent ideas to explore around here, unless you're especially hot to have company. Schumacher's overdue for some in-depth study. Where'd the Indian get the keys? From her or the now defunct Burnside?"

"I don't want contact with dispatch, just in case Pete's already pulled my badge. So you tell Mel where I'm going, all right? I'll check in with Mays' hospital switchboard from time to time. Fel's working there this week, and I know the receptionists. Leave word there if anything big breaks."

Tom nodded. "Meself will broadcast statewide a fervent request for Berendsi's head on a platter. We should smoke him out promptly." He tapped Joe's arm. "And one other thing, me chum. You're fooling no one but yourself if ye think that knot on your head's cleared up. Your headache might be better; ye seem more chipper; but your reaction time is nowhere near up to snuff. So allow for it, aye?"

"Yes, mother. Later." Joe settled into the seat of his Midget; it was almost too hot to sit on. He had the motor running when Gretchen came trotting out.

"Joe! Hold on!" She jogged up and leaned on the windshield post. "Sammie just called. Someone named Carol Murphy wants you to stop by. Didn't say where; just the name."

"On my way." Joe pulled away in the pleasant euphoria of having finally shed most of that blasted headache.

In a big way he hated stopping off here; in fact, he almost didn't. The depressing little apartment, the complex involvement with mixed-up people–he wanted to be on his way to what just might be the big piece in this puzzle. He knocked at Carol Murphy's door, in spite of himself.

She smiled as she let him in. "Wasn't sure the word would get to you. I just called a little bit ago."

Joe smiled and looked past her at the lanky young man near her. A brown-haired young man still wearing that black T-shirt.

His smile fled. "Robert Hawkins, I presume. That's the name you gave the city."

"Yeah. How'd you know?"

"We have your keys at headquarters."

The kid's face went blank and then he belatedly put two and two together. "That's why you came here earlier."

"No, though I somewhat suspected it was you. I'm Sergeant Joe Rodriguez."

"Can you sit? I need to talk to you."

Reluctantly Joe perched on a rickety chair. Hask/Hawkins flopped down across the table from him as if his chair were sturdy. He almost destroyed it. "I heard about the murder a couple minutes after it happened, on the radio. They didn't mention any names; they probably didn't know his name yet—he didn't carry ID usually—but I knew it was him. I knew it. So I got in my car right away and drove to the place the radio announcer said."

"And hung around watching. Watching what?"

Hask's head swayed. "I don't know. I couldn't believe it. I just stood there thinking about Loop getting snuffed in that spot and I couldn't believe it."

"When did you return here?"

"Late last night. Carol said you were here. Showed me your card. Said you mentioned a Hawkins. She didn't know about the Hawkins part—that

I use that name when I get a job. I even have a social security card in that name. She said I had to call you and straighten this out. She didn't know you cops were chasing me."

Should he take this kid down now, without backup, and risk hauling him into the office where Pete Marks was waiting to give him the boot? Or play it by ear here? Easy choice.

Joe sat back. His chair creaked. "It's always suspicious when a bystander hangs around an inordinately long time. We wanted to talk to you and you ran, creating more suspicion than we'd started with. What's the story?"

Hask looked helplessly at Carol. She dragged a chair in from the bedroom and plunked down on it. She licked her lips. "When you were talking to me them two times, uh, you seemed . . ." She groped for words. "You know, sensible."

"It's a compliment I may not deserve. Keep going."

"I want you to talk some sense into Bobby. He's . . . I don't know what to do. We been talking most of the night and now I'm as confused as he is."

Hask leaned both elbows on the table. It shook. "When I accepted Jesus at those Persis Magen meetings, I thought I had it all straightened out. And then Loop happened. Now I'm mixed up worse than ever. I didn't want Carol to call you, but then I thought why not, you know."

Joe sat forward cautiously. His chair was wiggling. "Carol said you and Loop argued. Start there and tell me about it."

"I told him what he was doing was wrong. And he said I was nuts because I didn't go for the big bucks any way I can. Anyway, the night before he, uh . . . he died, a couple hours, actually, he opened a can someplace on the north side. Took the stuff to Berendsi. Carol says you know about Berendsi. That was dumb. Five cents on a dollar, and he took it. That was dumb too. So he came over to our place afterward . . ."

"After he left Berendsi?"

"Yeah. He was in a fight—you know, an argument—with Berendsi. Berendsi let slip about a big job and I told Loop he oughta go to the police. Tell them. Then give up burglary and dealing and everything else and go straight." Hask swallowed.

"He took your advice and died violently a few hours later."

Hask nodded, tight-lipped.

"He was high when he came away from Berendsi's, right?"

Carol cut in. "We stripped the bathroom and locked him in it until he came down. When he was halfway normal, we let him out. It was almost dawn by then and Bobby had to go to work."

"Locked him in? I thought people in bathrooms locked other people out."

"We have a bolt on the outside of the door. Isn't the first time we locked somebody up 'cause they're too high to handle. Loop, either. It's nicer than the closet, and they have the toilet when they need it."

Hask stared at his hands on the jiggly table. "We took his money away from him and hid it too. We always do that till they come down. Loop understood. Anyway, before work that morning I finally convinced him he needed Jesus. Turn it all over to Jesus and start over. He did. He agreed. He accepted it. And he said he'd tell the cops what he knew. But he wanted the cops to give him a little something for the tip, you know? Promised he wouldn't buy anything but plain food with it."

"A fee for his information."

"Yeah. Right. I didn't see it would make any difference, you know, whether he tipped them for free or not. But then he said he couldn't just go to the cops without warning Berendsi, so Berendsi could back out if he didn't want to get caught. I never seen what he liked about Berendsi, or why he did business with him so much. But he did, I guess."

"Wait a minute." Joe's breastbone fluttered. "The morning he died, Loop went back to Berendsi?"

Carol added, "Yeah. It was after Bobby went to work. Seven-thirty maybe."

And Lu Ella didn't get up until past nine.

"You see?" Carol shuddered. "So now Bobby thinks if he hadn't preached to Loop, Loop would still be alive."

A rush of warm fuzzy feeling swept over Joe. He had a good solid answer for Bobby Hask, and Hask had added a piece to his puzzle. "First tell me this. Did Loop make a definite commitment to Jesus?"

"Yeah, but . . ." Hask frowned.

"No buts. Don't listen to what you're thinking, but to what I'm saying. Understand?"

A nod.

"When did Loop's eternal life begin? His salvation?"

"Right away, I guess. But. . . ."

"Did he say why he and Berendsi argued?"

"No. Money, I suppose. He was high, didn't make sense."

"Now listen to this: Loop had threatened to go to the police during the argument. He was going to sell his tip long before you suggested the idea to him. Do you understand? It was *not* your idea that sent him to his death."

"You don't know that."

"I *do* know that. Privileged testimony from other witnesses." Joe held up a hand and counted off fingers. First finger: "Loop was dissatisfied with Berendsi's offer." Second finger: "Berendsi boasted of a big haul coming in, hoping to cajole Loop into accepting less." Third finger: "Loop in turn threatened to take that information to the police, hoping to get a better deal." Pinky: "They argued hotly and Loop determined to carry out his threat." Joe thrust up his thumb. "The only reason Loop is not in hell right now is because you talked to him about Jesus between the time he left Berendsi and the time he tried to make contact with the police. You saved his spiritual life, and you're not responsible for the loss of his physical life." Joe sat back to let it sink in.

Hask gaped at him, transfixed. "Berendsi killed him then! He musta."

"Possibly. Possibly not. There are factors in this case I haven't mentioned."

"All right. But tell me when you catch the guy, will you? I wanna know."

"I will. Can you think of anything else that happened that day? Anything Loop did or said?"

They shook their heads in unison, but Joe approached the same question from a few other angles. He would phone Hask/Hawkins' return in to Mel and let Mel pick him up. Finally he stood up, anxious to be on his way. He felt good—almost elated. Carol Murphy and Robert Hask had just tied another knot in the noose that would hang Mouse's killer.

Whoever it was.

Reservation for Two

Joe watched the numbers on the gas pump spin. The Hopi and Navajo reservation had changed in one big way with the years. The gas pump here by the road was electric now. When Joe was young and his father brought him along up here, the pump was manual. With an old up-and-down pump handle, you forced gasoline into a glass tank in the top of the pump, then let gravity put it in your car. He could remember too when gas was 29 cents in town, which made the 48-cents-a-gallon reservation price look atrocious. The prices were still atrocious out here on the reservation.

The station attendant, a young Navajo, had already made the usual comments about the small sale. At most, the Midget took maybe five gallons. He gave the windshield one last swipe with the squeegee. "Got some blood?"

"Quarter Yaqui. You look like the real McCoy."

"Quarter white. I try to hide it."

Joe grinned. "Ready for this? I have a new wrinkle for the old cowboys-and-Indians game. I arrest the cowboys." He flipped his badge open. "Phoenix police."

"And you're chasing cowboys out here in Indian country?"

"Not this time. A Hopi possibly. Just a guess. Any major ceremonies out on the mesas lately?"

"Velvet Shirts finished up at Shungopavi a couple of days ago."

"Anything on First or Third Mesa?"

The boy leaned on the windshield frame. "They're trying to get one going at Oraibi, but they don't have enough dancers. Gotta borrow some from Second Mesa. Check your oil?"

"Did before I left. A middle-aged Anglo, five eight, balding, gray hair, fat, grouchy, hates Indians. Pontiac wagon."

The boy studied him. "Wanna make my whole day beautiful and tell me he's a cowboy you're gonna arrest?"

"He was by?"

"Pulled in just before noon with a bad carburetor. He acted like I was responsible for all his problems, so I turned Indian on him."

"Don't speak English, huh?"

The boy grinned. "Then he *really* got hostile. Turned purple. So I locked up the pumps and put out the CLOSED FOR LUNCH sign while he's standing there ranting. I mean, I don't take that kind of thing from nobody, man."

"He's having a bad day. Let me know if he comes by, will you? Even just driving past. I want to make his day a whole lot worse. But don't cross him. He's armed and dangerous."

"My pleasure. You might stop at Len's Chevron at Second Mesa. The wagon's gonna need help soon, the way it was sputtering. Len's sign sticks way up, easy to see. If he broke down, that's where he went."

"I'll do that." Joe fished out a card, scratched the office number and penciled in Mays'. "Here's the number. Dial direct and I'll pay you back. Dineh got any action going?"

"Pretty slow. A four-day way up at Kayenta in a month. Slow."

"I can imagine." Joe slid behind the wheel. "Especially when the electrical system's on the fritz in your truck."

The Navajo gaped. "How'd you know that?"

"That's got to be your truck out back there with the hood up. And you wouldn't get that acid burn on your hand messing with anybody's battery but your own. It's a disease, this being a detective. Good luck with your wiring."

He drove out onto the paved road. The sun bounced off the blacktop into his eyes, making the road look eternally wet in the distance. His headache returned.

He checked in at a pay phone outside the post office at Second Mesa. Tom had left no word via Mays, but a young woman had seemed anxious to find Joe. The hospital dispatcher had given her Tom's number. Carol Murphy again? Joe should have briefed Tom personally about his conversation with Robert Hask, instead of simply notifying Mel where the kid was.

A man answering Berendsi's description had spent several hours in Len's Chevron, fuming impatiently as his fuel filter, fuel line, and carburetor were being replaced. Joe was less than an hour behind him.

The Second Mesa area had changed tremendously in the last few years. New modern housing at the foot of the mesa had drained away both old and young. The old mesa-top village was virtually a ghost town. Not all was modern, though. A small boy sat under a tree near the road, splitting stovewood.

Joe parked on the berm and walked over. He had to crouch to get in the shade. The tree was less than fifteen feet high. "You split kindling about as fast as my boy does."

"How old is he?"

"Almost ten."

"Yeah? So'm I."

"I thought they had gas stoves here."

"Not the hornos. My aunt has to bake bread the old way. Says it doesn't taste right in a stove."

"I hear Velvet Shirts just finished up. You old enough to participate?"

He shook his head. "Dad says not yet."

"How'd it go?"

He shrugged amiably. "Okay. Some of the old ones were complaining the kachinas didn't pass around enough bread. One of the dancers got mixed up, couldn't concentrate. Dad says he didn't mess up ceremonially, though, so it was all right."

"Who? Do you know?"

The boy grinned. "They all look alike to me."

Joe wagged his head. "Too bad. That's why I came up. We thought he might have some bahana troubles; wanted to help him."

"He's got worries, all right, and they aren't all bahana, either. What's your kid's name?"

"Henry. We call him Rico. What's yours?"

"Charles. They call me Chip. Who wants to help him?"

"The outfit I work for down in Phoenix. We heard about him but we don't know his name."

"Carl Hobasie, at Shipaulovi."

Joe nodded. "Tell you what. The first gas-fired horno I hear about, Chip, I'll drop you a postcard. Save your pennies. No more kindling."

"All right!"

Joe ambled back to his car and waved to Chip under the tree, still chopping. Squatting in the shade awhile had helped his headache. It thudded yet but it didn't hurt.

He returned to the post office and checked in with Mays again. No word from Tom. He bought two cans of cola and stretched out for a few minutes under a piñon beyond the little brick post office. The MG overheated constantly, despite the modifications he had made in it over the years. He managed to get the front end of his car into the shade. Let it cool off.

A grasshopper leaped by his ear, churred and disappeared in the dust. His mind drifted. He thought of Marie who would be coming out here in a few months. He'd take some annual leave and help her hunt for an apartment. Marie. She sang, she floated, she teased on his drowsy mind.

He had promised her he would try to grow spiritually. His prayer life was zilch, his Bible reading similarly zero. The odd hours he was working, he didn't even get to church. She would be sadly disappointed. He hated that.

A familiar soprano voice warbled, "There he is!" but Joe was too near asleep to react quickly. He lurched to sitting as something thunked across the hood of his car.

She lay sprawled on her tummy just in front of his windshield, her elbows on the fender. Her cleavage gaped prominently through the gap in the low neckline of her tank top. She grinned and raised one hand palm outward in the stereotype Indian gesture of greeting.

"How!" said Bernice.

"And tuck your shirttail in." Joe waited by his car door as Bernice made herself presentable. The blue tank top still showed through her blouse, and if her short shorts were any shorter her belly button would have been hanging out. Lascivious.

"Now am I fit to be seen with you?"

"Better."

"But you're still mad at me. I didn't think I cared whether you were mad, but I do. Well, a little."

"It was a fool stunt! How'd you get that United Parcel driver to bring you here, anyway? It's strictly illegal."

She lifted her hands helplessly. "He certainly

wasn't going to let this poor little white girl walk down the road all alone in this heat, was he?"

"But how did you get up here to the reservation?"

"I have this friend who's going for his pilot's license. He has to log so many hours in the air and I wanted a fast lift to the res."

Joe turned on his heel and started along the rocky path. "I'm going to strangle Tom Flaherty." On his right, the ancient adobe walls of Shipaulovi glowed in the late afternoon sun. On his left, the mesa fell away before endless, timeless desert and lucid sky.

"It wasn't Tom's fault. Bet he doesn't even realize he let slip where you were." She huddled in close against him. "I've been to a dozen foreign countries, but I feel more like an outsider here than anyplace in Europe."

"You are one. How'd you walk right up to me? Lawrence Dobbs on the beat again?"

"Your little sports car sticks out like a bagpipe player in the Philadelphia Symphony, among all these pickup trucks. The driver had to stop at Second Mesa anyway, and there you were."

Joe stopped and glanced around. "You stand against this wall here. Right here. Understand?"

"What if your criminal or whatever is inside there?"

"That's why you stay right here. You'll be safe if things start popping. And no lip. You do as you're told, hear?"

The door he wanted stood open, so he rapped on the jamb. A gentle womanly voice bade him enter. He stepped out of glare into gloom. All he could think of for a moment was the jeopardy of this temporary blindness. He should have closed his eyes a minute before knocking.

"Mrs. Hobasie?"

"Yes."

"Joe Rodriguez. I'm looking for Carl Hobasie."

"He's not here just now. You may wait, if you wish. It will be awhile." Gray-haired and heavyset, she sat at her table in the gloom, quietly picking through a pile of beans. Even in a plain cotton housedress she looked as regal and dignified as the Queen Mother. And sad. "Sit down if you like."

The place was two rooms, this one and a bedroom. Joe sat facing the second room. Tom was right about his head; this whole day was starting to wear very hard. He hauled out his badge and held it for her. "Phoenix police. I'd like to ask your husband some questions."

"It must be very important; you came up here."

"I grab any chance I can to come up here." A silversmithing bench lined the wall beside him, its tools and torch neatly arranged. "The postmistress says you're as fine a silversmith as your husband."

"She always says that, but it's not true."

"You do some silver work?"

"I just make a little piece now and then from Carl's scraps. A little money, you know?"

"Your husband isn't the artist who made Otis Burnside's rings?"

"Yes. Many years ago, when he worked at the museum."

"Why did your husband leave his job at the museum?"

"They asked him to stay, but this is home, not Phoenix. All our generations live here—the ones alive and the ones dead. He wasn't happy there."

"Your husband knows Vale Schumacher too?"

"Yes. He knew her a long, long time, before she took Mr. Burnside's place."

Joe's neck prickled. "Took his place? How do you mean?"

"He was the head man. She was a famous professor. Scientist. And they gave her a new fancy title, and put her at the top. Carl says it was for prestige—the museum's prestige—to have a famous professor. It hurt Mr. Burnside, Carl says, very much. But he got over it. The museum did start paying everyone more after she came. Carl earned more. But then he left."

"Do she and your husband still maintain contact? Write, phone, talk to each other?"

"She was here just this afternoon."

"Here!"

Mrs. Hobasie looked mildly perplexed. "Is that wrong?"

"No. Not at all. Just surprising."

"She asked where she might find him, but I made a mistake. I thought he was going to talk to Rassah. After I sent her off I remembered he's not going to go there until tomorrow. I sent her in the wrong direction. When she comes back, she can wait here or I'll send her in the right direction, as she likes."

"Joe?" Bernice's voice whined. "I'm getting hot."

Joe sighed heavily.

"Your wife, Mr. Rodriguez?"

"Not even my girlfriend. May she come in?"

The lady tittered, bemused. "Of course."

Bernice popped in the door before Joe could stand up. "It's roasting out there. I was afraid my spit would curdle."

"How about sitting down quietly right there, Bernice." Joe pointed toward a chair well aside of the bedroom door.

Bernice paused, squeezing her eyes shut. She headed for her appointed place and stopped cold in the bedroom doorway. "What a beautiful girl." She turned to Mrs. Hobasie. "Is that your daughter? The picture on the table in there? She's lovely."

"Yes, she is. Thank you." The sadness in her voice welled to the surface and overflowed.

Obviously Bernice saw it too. She abandoned her assigned chair and plopped down on a stool at Mrs. Hobasie's elbow. "Did something happen to her?"

"I shouldn't discuss it with strangers."

"Oh." Bernice nodded. "Yeah, I guess we're strangers. Well, if your husband really doesn't want you to. . . ."

"It's not that. I shouldn't burden you, is all."

Joe started picking through beans. "My grandmother must have spent a third of her lifetime sorting through beans. Either that or adding water to them on the stove." He glanced up. "I didn't hear about your daughter. I'd like to, if it's not prying."

"Yeah," Bernice echoed. "That's her school picture, right? Her senior picture?"

"Yes, but she didn't finish her senior year yet." Her warm dark eyes watched Joe's hands move. "We have three sons and this one daughter. She has a disease; I can't remember the name. Doctor's words are so hard to remember."

Joe smiled. "I've heard a doctor say that about Hopi words."

She smiled. "They took her by plane to Phoenix for special treatments. Even so, she might die."

"Bummer! You mean you couldn't go along?" Bernice for once in her life seemed genuinely interested in somebody besides herself. "Wish you could remember the disease."

Joe wagged his head. "And on top of it all, the cost."

"Yes. The cost. Carl says he's taking care of it, and the tribal council is helping. I'm not to worry about it."

"In what way is he taking care of it? Did he say?"

"I don't know. He went to Phoenix a couple of weeks ago to make arrangements, he says. He's doing some work for someone. Good money in it."

"Did he mention any names?"

"No."

"For the museum? Working for them again?"

"I don't think so. He would have said."

"Does he seem pleased with the payment?"

"He did at first. But early this morning when he came back from the second trip he was upset. I guess it's not quite as much as he thought." She scooped the beans off the table into a bowl.

"It will probably be easiest if I go find him and talk to him. You say you remember where he's gone?"

"To tend his hives."

"Hives?"

"Carl keeps bees. It's a nice bit of side income.

His hives are on a little mesa across the road. The Apache plume is blooming there now. Good honey from Apache plume."

Joe stood up. "May I look at your daughter's picture?"

"Of course."

Joe walked back into the bedroom to look at the photo closely—also to assure himself that Carl Hobasie was not here. Bernice was right; the photo showed a bright and lovely young lady.

He paused in the door and wiggled a finger toward Bernice. "Mrs. Hobasie, what kind of truck does he drive?

"His truck? He's driving his team and wagon."

Joe nodded. "Thank you, Mrs. Hobasie. God bless you." With Bernice at his heels he stepped from cool dark gloom into the golden brilliance of a Hopi afternoon. The land is so lovely when it's not tarnished by men's evil.

A Case of Hives

Of all the unique little corners that enrich Arizona and nowhere else, Joe liked the mesas best. From the ragged tableland of the Four Corners, a series of narrow mesas, like fingers in a carelessly dropped glove, thrust themselves out into the high desert north of the rim. Ancient mud-hut villages in a constant state of repair and disrepair perch atop their steep cliffs.

Roads, a mere afterthought in the pattern of the land, wander here and there as the need arises. Present but a few hundred years in the mesas' ancient book of days, Anglo interlopers have tucked their trading posts and gas stations in what they think to be convenient places. Cornfields and squash patches that would hardly be recognized by a Midwest farmer nestle in corners dictated by the laws of geology and drainage. Endless wind and tireless sun and seasonal rain all march to the secret rhythms of the kachinas, the spirits of everything good and evil in the Hopi world.

Haunting and compelling as this wide land might be, it had its faults, and the road Mrs. Hobasie sent Joe on was a major one. Here wound a track in worse shape than that trace back to the petroglyphs. He hadn't been thinking when he left Phoenix. He should have taken the time to go back to Tempe and get the 'Burb, lousy mileage and all. His little Midget with its five-inch clearance was no match for reservation tracks. When a wide spot happened along, he turned the Midget around and backed up until the ruts got too deep. When a foot-high rut turned out to be the shallowest, he abandoned driving. He'd walk to the mesa crest.

Like a bored puppy, Bernice fell in behind. "We're not having quite as much pure fun as I thought we would."

"I don't want to hear about it."

This was a pretty little flattop hill. Its sides dropped away steeply in places, nearly vertically in others, quite gently out toward its tip. It wore its crown of frosted, shrubby Apache plume only slightly askew.

Joe had climbed almost to the top when he stopped so abruptly Bernice bumped into him. He dropped to a squat and yanked her down to her knees.

He whispered hoarsely, "If Hobasie had been hiding in that bedroom feeling cornered, you could have lost your pretty little head a few minutes ago, do you realize that?"

"Yeah, but he wasn't."

"Right. Because he's just ahead up there. And a man who may have murdered two people is with him. I know that man is carrying a Luger. You'll stay down. Flat down. You keep your head below these rocks, no matter what you see or hear. We're playing for keeps now. Understand?"

Her marvelous eyes grew larger. She settled against the dry and stony slope. "I'll be good."

"If you act responsibly only once in your life, this is the time." He pulled his gun as he stepped away from her. He moved crouching along the rim until the sharp mesa edge gave way to a gentle roll. He wanted to hear—to eavesdrop—but the sparse desert brush provided scant cover.

Berendsi was waving his pistol in Hobasie's face. Joe could hear the louder parts of the tirade—threats of holes and being torn apart. The Pontiac was parked over beyond the white wooden boxes that were the hives, and how Berendsi got that road monster up here Joe had no idea. The rickety wagon and team of aged roan horses standing beside it must have had a hard enough time reaching the top.

Berendsi's distraught voice came through in strident snatches—there hadn't been enough, not nearly enough. Accept what was offered or . . .

Hobasie spotted Joe behind the partial cover of a lacy creosote bush. Berendsi wheeled to stare. With a frustrated howl he shoved the Indian aside and dashed for the Pontiac. He totally ignored Joe's suggestion to freeze.

The station wagon lunged forward, covering the

horses in a billow of dust. Berendsi switched from right- to left-handed and thrust his gun out his open window. Both the Luger and the Pontiac were pointed at Joe now.

Joe put a bullet through the radiator, not necessarily on purpose. White steam boiled out. The Luger bucked and bucked again, its noise all but swallowed up in the general confusion. Joe flattened a front tire. The vehicle swerved, waggled and came at him again. *Quit being nice, you idiot.* Joe put two through the windshield where Berendsi ought to have been. The Pontiac was on him now, its three good tires roaring in the soft caliche. Joe dived over the side, slid and skidded down the steep, loose dirt bank as Berendsi's car howled past.

He tried to arrest his slide short of the bottom and could not. By the time he regained his feet he was much too far below the track to get another shot at the car. He turned his attention to Hobasie.

The Indian was whipping his horses to a dead run, coming off the mesa by a back road. As desperately as Berendsi was trying to escape west, Hobasie was headed northeast. Joe raced off across the stony flat, cutting the corner. If he could just reach that open stretch of back road before Hobasie did. . . .

Joe and Hobasie arrived at the same point at about the same moment. Joe leveled his gun on the terrified Hopi, yelled at him to stop. The Indian lashed his horses all the harder. Shooting at Berendsi was one thing, but this was quite another. Joe couldn't bring himself to hurt the panic-stricken, trouble-beset man in his sights now. He leaped aside as the wagon clattered past, nearly running him down.

He dropped to sitting for long moments and watched the wagon's dust cloud move in slow motion across the desert. He would have slammed his gun into the dirt in frustration, but he didn't have the energy. His clothes and body were soaking wet, his legs trembling, his head pounding. The heat was getting him. Living his whole life in Phoenix did not immunize him to the danger in this desert summer. He should have been more prudent. Now he had to get back to Bernice, to shade, to rest. The horizon wavered lazily in a nauseating sine curve.

"Joe?" The voice was Marie's, floating across the open waste. He struggled to his feet and nearly fell over. It was not Marie. Bernice came running out across the flat toward him, red-faced. "Joe!" She was slick with sweat. She practically knocked him over as she wrapped her arms around his waist. "I couldn't do anything! I'm so sorry. I couldn't do anything."

Joe pretended to hold her. Actually he was leaning on her, his head too giddy to keep him upright. "Let's go find some shade."

"You look terrible. Here. Take a drink first. I was too scared to think, but I did remember to grab this." She handed him one of those big oasis water bags. "It was hanging on the back bumper of his station wagon."

Joe stared at the bag, his brain in neutral. "This isn't mine."

She pressed her lips together. "I have some good

news and some bad news. The good news is, we have lots of water here. The bad news is, he abandoned his car and hot-wired yours for his getaway."

"How are you feeling now?" Bernice's voice startled him from drowsiness to alertness. "You looked ready to croak an hour ago."

"Fine. You?" Joe opened his eyes. They were going to have to move in a few minutes. The waning sun would soon chase off this bit of shade they were stretched out in.

"Dandy." She flipped over onto her elbows, her warm body snuggled against his. "So what's next?"

"Walk back to Second Mesa, round up Hobasie and tell all the world about Berendsi. Highway Patrol should have him collared by dark."

She nodded. "How come you didn't reload your gun yet?"

"The reload's under the seat of the Midget."

"Guess that'll do for an excuse." She pushed in closer. "Wanna come along up to my room?" She didn't wait for his answer. She leaned out and kissed him. Her lips nestled, soft and moist and remarkably cool. He knew he should be resisting this, for any number of reasons, but he didn't have the strength to resist. Soft messages of *This is totally wrong, pal* failed to get through.

Involuntarily he rolled toward her, wrapped an arm around her, pressed down upon her. The world tiptoed quietly away.

The kiss lasted only for a minute or two, as did the quiet. The sound of a motor forced itself to the edge of his awareness. It was a familiar motor too, with a little wheeze where the sixth cylinder should have been firing. He disconnected and propped himself up on one elbow.

Bernice muttered her disgust and flopped back.

Joe grinned and sat up, watching Rocinante lurch and heave and claw its way along the choppy track.

"I take it," mumbled Bernice, "that this is some clown's version of the cavalry coming to the rescue."

"With an Irish John Wayne." Joe stood up as Rocinante snuffled to an asthmatic halt. He was so happy to see Tom he held the door open for him.

Tom came bobbing out, his spirits nowise wilted by the heat, and waved a six-pack of cola aloft. "Be that an infamous Pontiac wagon I see in the far distance?"

"With a ruined wheel rim and a deep-fried engine. It's gone as far as it's going to go."

"We suspected as much. So he came up here."

"And left again."

"Oh? We didn't pass him on the way, but that doesn't mean a thing. We stopped for an iced tea, Dr. Schumacher and meself."

Dr. Schumacher climbed stiffly out of the passenger side. "We should have brought my Land Rover, Mr. Flaherty. At least it has a suspension system." She stretched.

Tom nodded toward Bernice. "So here ye be. Your darling mama be worried witless, lass."

"Don't count on it." Bernice lay back and closed her eyes.

"Happy to see you're your usual charming self."

Tom folded up in the meager shade and handed her two cans. She passed one on to Joe.

Joe settled near Tom, Bernice between them, and popped his can open. "We're 400 miles from home on an unmaintained road two feet from hell. How'd you manage to find us?"

Bernice stretched out fetchingly and closed her eyes. She drew one leg up languidly to half cock. "Deductive reasoning, Jose, me lad. You're after Carl Hobasie, am I right?"

"I have a new respect for deductive reasoning. Tell me more."

Tom hesitated a moment, unconsciously surveying the smooth line of Bernice's leg. "Dr. Schumacher and I worked it out. How might the thief have obtained keys? A: He was or is an employee. B: He's a friend, relative, or blackmailer of same. I set Harry and Ginger to B and pursued A personally."

Dr. Schumacher squeezed in under the edge of the speckled shade. "We make a point of employing Indians whenever possible, so there were quite a few names to check. I'm certain you've zeroed in on the wrong man. I know Hobasie. This isn't him."

Tom continued. "Three Apaches and two Hopis approximated the physical description of our fleet-of-foot perp, and of the two Hopis, Hobasie fits the bill. The other be in his late seventies."

"How old is Hobasie, anyway, Tommy?"

"Ready for this? Fifty-nine, and he outran the both of us, with a weight handicap yet. Mother Carey's nightgown! Would that I be so well preserved in me old age. And here's a clincher:

Hobasie was one of the workmen who installed the very cases that were burglarized, and three of the pieces stolen are his own silver work."

"I feel sorry for him." Bernice flipped over on her side and ran her finger lazily up and down Joe's arm. It bothered him, and no doubt she knew it.

"So do I," Joe agreed. "His first trip to Phoenix was two weeks ago. That's when he set everything up, including Berendsi. Cased the museum to make sure it was the way he remembered it."

Schumacher shook her head. "Why not commit the deed then? If it were he, why did he wait?"

"The kiva ceremonies. He had to be here, and he had to be unsoiled by such a gross wrongdoing. As soon as he completed his responsibilities here, he headed back down."

Bernice snapped to sitting. "I don't understand how you found us clear out here. Mrs. Hobasie tell you?"

Tom smiled smugly. "In a strange area, where's the three best places to find practical information?"

"I don't know, three times."

"Your local gas station, your local beauty salon, and the postmaster. In this case, postmistress. Ye might pass that along to your neophyte gumshoe."

"He'll be thrilled with this tip from a pro."

"No doubt." Tom opened a fresh pack of cigarettes. "We narrowed the possibles to Hobasie, whose only address was a Second Mesa box number, so I stopped here soon as I arrived; had some matters to clear up at the office first." He offered cigarettes all around but only Bernice reached for one. He rapped her knuckles as he yanked the pack away. "The postmistress remembered seeing Hobasie drive by in his wagon and gave us general directions here."

"And you?" Joe looked at Schumacher. "You came with him?"

"I came up independently. My Rover's parked at the post office. I made the decision after Detective Flaherty left my office. I found where Hobasie lived; he moved since I was last up here; but Mrs. Hobasie was mistaken as to where her husband had gone. I couldn't find him. But I did bump into the detective."

"Why come up here at all?" Joe finished off his cola.

"Present company excepted, of course, I didn't trust the police to do something I can do better myself—recovering my silver if it's here. Different jurisdictions and all that. I couldn't picture the tribal police getting enthusiastic about recovering museum silver."

"And what about that altercation between you and Sommers that we interrupted?"

The sudden change of topic failed to unhorse her. She didn't hesitate. "Some of the petroglyphs we found were on rocks small enough for two people to manage. He wanted to take them home for private profit. I was adamant. So was he. Apparently he had some sort of market in mind—someone's patio, no doubt."

"And he was greedy enough to leave you behind, at least long enough to teach you an economics lesson. For the sake of some chipped rocks?"

"Chipped rocks." She grimaced.

"I wonder how extensive his market connections were. When I caught him at the museum–"

"When *we* caught him," Bernice corrected.

"When we caught him at the museum, he probably had a market all set up, perhaps even for specific pieces."

"I'm bored." Bernice flattened out on her back again, dropped one knee and raised the other.

Tom drained his second cola. "You're pensive again, Joe."

Joe stared at the dust on his boots. "Couple things don't click and I can't see what they are. They keep slipping away. Something that doesn't gel, something I should be seeing."

"Something old, something new, something borrowed, something blue, and no, I don't want to get married." Bernice hopped to her feet. "But I'll be happy to consider a live-in situation with you. Let's move."

Schumacher stood up. "The girl does have a point; we're accomplishing nothing sitting here."

Joe stood up. He ached all over and his head felt thick and heavy yet. "Gimme your reload, Tommy. Mine's in the Midget."

"And where, might I ask, is the Midget?"

"On its way to Phoenix, I suppose. Berendsi borrowed it."

"Must be perdition for ye." Tom flopped in behind Rocinante's wheel and stretched to unlock the glove compartment. Joe held the back door open and Schumacher slid in, but Bernice bounced into the front seat. Joe was too spent to argue. He plopped down beside her and shut the door. He slammed it three times more. The latch finally held.

Tom handed him the soft plastic holder and ground the starter. Rocinante heaved itself into reverse and jolted backward toward some wide spot to turn around in.

Bernice cupped her hands below his gun, so he dumped the cylinder there and slipped in the reload. "Tommy, the way Mrs. Hobasie talked, she knows nothing about any of this. I think Carl kept her in the dark."

Schumacher leaned forward. "You're saying the silver isn't there?"

"I doubt it." He leaned back in his favorite position and by habit draped his arm along the seat back. Bernice apparently mistook it as a gesture of affection. She curled up against him. She was distracting enough to keep him away from those nagging little somethings that simply would not click.

Busy as a Bee

Something was up in Shipaulovi pueblo. That open spot where Joe had parked a few hours earlier with lots of room to spare was now filled with not one but three vehicles – an Arizona Highway Patrol cruiser, a County Sheriff's vehicle, and a tribal police pickup truck. Tom squeezed Rocinante in between the pickup and an adobe wall. They had to wiggle to crawl out the doors.

The sun was drifting earthward in one of those glorious golden evenings that make the Four Corners country so spectacular, and Joe paused a moment on the lip of the mesa to admire the view. Harsh desert stretched in deceptively gentle rolls from here to infinity.

Bernice brushed against his arm. "If you're so incurably romantic, how come I can't seduce you?"

"I won't dignify that with an answer." He latched

onto her elbow and piloted her around the corner toward the Hobasie apartment. Tom loudly suppressed a giggle.

People crowded the dark, stifling Hobasie apartment like kids around the ice-cream truck. Joe rapped on the jamb but no one noticed him. He stepped inside. In addition to the badges represented by the vehicles outside were several elders and not a few women. The place was packed.

A highway patrolman glanced up. "Who're you?"

Joe presented his badge, despite that they were a dime a dozen here, and introduced his party mechanically. Carl Hobasie was not one of the many people standing about in this room; Joe had to crane his neck a bit to make certain. "We're looking for a Carl Hobasie."

The patrolman smiled. He was slim, tall, and a decade younger than Joe. He nodded toward the ladies and extended his hand. "Jim Kendall. What does Phoenix Metro want with Hobasie?"

"We suspect him of complicity in a—"

Bernice's gasp cut him off. She shoved between two burly elders and dropped down to her knees beside an overstuffed chair. Concealed behind the many onlookers, Mrs. Hobasie sat numb and listless, staring straight ahead. Bernice took the lady's hand and held it. Just held it.

Kendall bobbed his head toward the chair. "Mrs. Hobasie just got hit with a ton of bricks."

"Her daughter died?" Joe could feel the heaviness.

"Oh, you knew about that? Yeah. The elders were coming up the hill to tell her when they heard gunshots. Before they could reach the top, a little sports car comes roaring down; almost hits them. They find that some fat guy ransacked the place here; you see the mess; pushed the missus around and shot Hobasie when he walked in on it and put up a fight."

Joe's head spun. "Carl Hobasie's dead?"

"Yeah. Instantly. It happened so fast nobody got a license number or a clear description. All the elders can tell us is that it was a sports car with the top down."

So the ghosts and monsters reached far beyond the dark nights and Yaqui campfires.

The enormity of it smothered Joe. It took him a minute to gather enough words in one place to speak. "The car's a green '67 MG Midget, Arizona 853 VCQ. I'm the owner of record. Driver's John Berendsi. We already put out an all-points statewide, car and driver both."

"You have answers, I have questions. Come on outside."

Joe pulled away from Kendall without really hearing. He dropped down beside Bernice. "Mrs. Hobasie?"

The lady turned her dark eyes to him. She had aged thirty years in the last few hours. "The medicine isn't so strong that I don't remember you, Mr. Rodriguez. You're too late to talk to Carl."

Someone at Joe's shoulder was explaining something about sedation. Joe laid his hand on hers. "Mrs. Hobasie, did the fat man leave here with anything?"

"I don't think so. Carl. I didn't see exactly. No.

She was my only daughter."

Bernice sobbed. Tears flowed copiously down her face.

Joe had no idea what to say, but one of the odd pieces that would not click suddenly fell into place. "I don't know what it's like to lose a daughter, but I have one; I know what it's like to love one. I'm very sorry."

She rotated her wrist and gave his hand a little squeeze. Joe squeezed back and stood up. Rage—rage and anger and frustration—blinded him. He could have stopped this, had he only seen it coming. And he *should* have seen it. He shoved past Kendall, shouldered past Tom, slammed his way out the door. A small parade followed him out—the patrolman, Bernice and Schumacher, Tom. . . . He walked beyond earshot of the door to a broken wall near the vehicles. He must not further disturb the stricken Mrs. Hobasie.

He wheeled on Tom and exploded. "Hang it, Tommy, why didn't I see it? If I'd only stayed with Hobasie—with his wagon—I could have prevented all this! He'd still be alive. I had a round left!"

Tom grabbed his shoulders and shook. "Stop it! Your yowling will bring in cats from thirty miles around. Get a grip on yourself. Settle down and start from the beginning."

Kendall and a tribal policeman both spoke, but Joe ignored them. He concentrated on Tommy's face, Tommy's strong and familiar face . . . get his wits gathered back together. He took a deep breath. "Berendsi and Hobasie were out at Hobasie's bee hives. When they spotted me, Berendsi took the logical escape route—out to the main road. But Hobasie went the other way, Tom."

"So?"

"He wasn't trying to get away from me. Berendsi was the threat, not me. He ignored me. And I was right behind him. If I'd kept going—followed his wagon back here—I could have reached here not long after he did. Protected him from Berendsi."

"Only one round left? Ye would've got your darling head blown off."

Joe wheeled away and slapped the warm sandpapery adobe with his palm. "Berendsi didn't get any silver from Hobasie. I should have realized immediately that he'd come straight back here. Come here to search the most logical place first. Instead I glibly assumed he'd leave the area. How could I be so stupid?"

Bernice seized his arm and yanked him around to face her. "You big dope. You almost dropped over from the heat! You even had to lean on me. You wouldn't have lasted fifty feet trying to chase that wagon!" The waning sun set her hair to glowing like new copper.

It dawned like a light, gleamed like the setting sun behind him. Joe saw it now. "Gimme the keys! Come on!" He ran for Rocinante, the parade at his heels. "Bernice, you stay here."

"Bet you can't make me!" She dived into the backseat before Joe could get the engine started. He had no time to argue. Schumacher piled in beside Bernice. Tom slammed the right door and slammed it and slammed it and slammed it.

Joe backed out with a squeal. Rocinante's bumper thunked into the cruiser's fender with a soft *whupp*. He swung around and roared down the hill twenty miles an hour faster than he ought. Behind him came the highway patrolman and the tribal cop—two sets of headlights.

"Tommy, find Kendall on the radio."

Tom lifted the mike and began exploring channels.

"Found 'm, Jose."

Joe took the mike. "Kendall, I'm taking a back road to a little mesa behind the Hewitt place. I'm certain our man went there. You swing out front, past Hewitts' and come in from the main road to head him off. He'll try to escape out that way. Know where I mean?"

"No. Hewitt? Huh? What's going on here?"

The tribal policeman, "I know where he means, Jim. Follow me."

They parted company at the bottom of the mesa. The two vehicles howled off down the main highway and Joe swung around in the shadow of the hill. He found the back road with difficulty in this waning light, but he killed his headlights anyway. Headlights make inviting targets. Rocinante bucked like a mechanical bull along the ruts. Joe glanced behind. They were raising a great wall of dust.

Tom gripped the dash. "You're a maniac on these goat tracks!"

Bernice hooked her elbows over the seat, her soft face inches from his ear. "This Berendsi is who killed the role model, right? So where does Mrs. Hobasie's husband fit?"

"I see it." Tom's knuckles on the dash were

white. "With his usual miserly attitude, Berendsi wasn't willing to give Hobasie full value, so Hobasie held out. Wouldn't let him have the goodies he'd been counting on so fervently."

"That's right," Joe agreed. "Hobasie needed enough to cover some heavy medical expenses. With Berendsi it was business; to Hobasie it was life or death."

"Eh," Tom nodded. "Hobasie being a master silversmith in his own right, he could alter the museum marks on the Hopi pieces and sell them as his own work for a much better price than Berendsi was offering. Thus he stole Hopi pieces selectively."

"Berendsi wasn't going to let that trove slip through his fingers, so he came up here to take it by force, if necessary."

"But where are we going?" Bernice bounced sideways into him and recovered her balance. "The only thing out here is his dead Pontiac and a bunch of old beehives. What would—oh wow! Yeah!"

"Yeah what?" Tom braced himself between seat and dash.

Her soprano voice warbled with enthusiasm and the jolting. "The beehives! Greatest place in the world to hide silver. Nobody'd try to look in there, right, Joe?"

"Right." But the picture still wasn't complete. A major piece refused to fall in line, and Joe couldn't see the whole puzzle to save him. His head was roaring again, the headache compounded by the heat and this jolting road.

Tom pointed toward distant lights. "Kendall and the tribal cop are out to the main highway. And there be a third set of lights with them; sheriff perhaps. Or mayhap 'tis a confused tourist who just loves a parade."

"Or the FBI," Schumacher offered. "They have jurisdiction in Hobasie's death . . . if they've been notified."

Joe calculated briefly. "We'll reach Berendsi long before they get to the mesa. Bernice, keep your head down, hear me? Below window level. You too, Dr. Schumacher."

"And miss all the fun?" Bernice hooted. "What'll I get if I cooperate?"

"It's what you'll get if you don't, Twerp. Possibly a stray bullet. Berendsi's really wired; he'll be hard to take."

"Twerp? You call all your girlfriends Twerp?"

"I don't call any of my girlfriends Twerp. And put on your seatbelt!"

"This is great. Maybe I'll go partners with Lawrence."

The right door clunked and fell open. "Now you've done it!" Tom grabbed it, tried to hold it closed.

Rocinante began the steep climb to the mesa top. It fishtailed and nearly ground to a stop as its wheels spun helplessly in loose dirt. It caught on something solid as it sideslipped. It lurched forward again.

As they topped out, Berendsi wheeled toward them. He was surrounded by parts and pieces of beehives all ashambles. Tom yelled "Down!" as the Luger swung toward them. Joe ducked, killed the motor, hit the brake. Rocinante skidded to a stop as the windshield shattered. The tires on his Midget had less than 5,000 miles on them—he was going to hate to shoot them out. Tom rolled out onto the gravel.

Wild-eyed, Berendsi fired one more with that Luger and gave the whole thing up. He tossed his gun aside and dropped face down in the dust.

Tom swung wide to approach Berendsi from the far side, his gun leveled two-handed on the trembling pawnbroker. "It gives me great pleasure to wrap this one up, Jose, me lad. Satisfying!"

Satisfying? No. Joe wasn't satisfied. This was wrong; it was all wrong; but he didn't know what was right. This somehow wasn't the exact fit and his headache wouldn't let him shift pieces to find the right fit. He sidestepped ten feet and reached for the Luger, his eyes on Berendsi.

The Luger was lying right there under his fingertips. With a poof it was gone, snatched from beneath his outstretched hand. He snapped erect as a flurry of action blurred behind him.

Schumacher looked murderously competent at handling the Luger. She held it level, her finger on the trigger. "I'll blow a hole through you. And she'll go first, I swear."

All the pieces came into place. He could see the picture clearly now... now that it might be too late.

Joe heard Tom's gun go *plip* in the dirt. He flicked his own gun away near the base of a nearby beehive, within reach should he make it to cover.

Schumacher's voice crackled like dry leaves. "You. Berendsi. Don't lie there like a stupid donkey. Let's go!"

Still sprawled in the dust, he raised his head to stare at her.

"I need you and you need me. Together we can get out of this and take a nice little nest egg with us. Come on; step on it! We'll take this old prowl car. I know the back roads. And with any luck we can drive right past those three cars coming in."

Berendsi needed no second invitation to reprieve. He scrambled to his feet.

"No, John! Wait!" Joe held out a hand toward him. Berendsi hesitated. "She killed Loop and Mouse in cold blood. Don't think she won't shoot you down along with the rest of us. You touch silver and you're a dead man."

Schumacher yelled at him; her icy surface was cracking.

Joe kept his voice mellow. "How many rounds left in the Luger, John?"

"Five. No. Four."

Joe turned to the museum maven. "Then you can't afford to miss even once, Schumacher. Better take out Tom and me first. We're the most dangerous. On the other hand, you don't want to excite Berendsi's suspicions prematurely. Let him come up with some of the silver first, to make your own story more convincing."

"What story?" Berendsi eyed her.

Schumacher waved that gun. "Move, you idiot! We only have a few minutes before the others get here."

"What others?" Berendsi glanced around.

With a howl to scare banshees, Tom dived sideways across the hood of the Midget; Joe heard his belt buckle growl, metal on metal, across the width of it. Schumacher fired wildly at Tom as he disappeared safely beyond the car. One shell gone. Already Joe was flinging himself behind a partly dismantled beehive. He snatched for his gun and missed.

He grabbed the nearest thing, a shattered, dripping frame of honeycomb, popped up and hurled it, bees and all, at Schumacher.

He dropped down again and made another vain, groping lunge for his gun. Schumacher screeched; the Luger roared. Two spent.

This was not the most propitious of moments, but Joe seized it anyway. He knocked the beehive aside and lunged at Schumacher. He'd done a good job with the honeycomb; bees and goo covered Schumacher's eyes. He grabbed her gun arm somewhere around the elbow without slowing. He drove forward; she collapsed backward, and he landed on top of her. For the very first time in his life, Joe Rodriguez punched a woman—as hard as he could.

Tom was yelling something. Joe rolled to his feet and wheeled, but Tom had it all under control. John Berendsi stood frozen. He stared at Tom and Tom stared back. Tom waggled the muzzle of his own sidearm. Berendsi resigned himself to the obvious and bellied out again spread-eagle.

Joe felt just a tiny twinge about snapping the cuffs on Schumacher. Now she couldn't brush away the bees. Already her eyes and cheeks were starting to swell.

Berendsi snarled, "It was a trick—and I fell for it."

"No trick, John. You saved your own life."

Tom wagged his head as he cuffed the pawnbroker. "This whole scene's a wee bit confusing, Joe. Enlighten me."

"When I first talked to Schumacher beyond Bapchule, she assumed Loop and Mouse died simultaneously, felled in their tracks. Also, she assumed the tipster was a man. But I couldn't remember saying anything that would have given her that information. Was she guessing, making idle assumptions, or did she know more than she ought?

"She probably discovered Burnside's chicanery weeks ago. Perhaps even months ago. She must keep the museum's reputation spotless at all costs. Should they become known, Burnside's shenanigans would dry up future contributions, and would surely cause contributors to pull any on-loan pieces. All sorts of bad ramifications. Hobasie was the perfect foil, Berendsi the perfect fence. Once the museum was robbed and the pieces started turning up elsewhere, its reputation was safe again. Whatever was missing could be chalked off to a tragic theft. The museum accrues sympathy, not distrust."

"Now that ye mention it, she was more a hindrance than a help digging names out of the file. 'Twas her secretary—that receptionist—who helped best. Hobasie worked for the museum years ago; she probably met him then or even before, as a field researcher. But how'd she tie in with Berendsi?"

"I never met her!" Berendsi yelped.

Joe looked at the prostrate felon. "Probably not until she needed you to distribute Hobasie's loot.

She bought an occasional piece of hot silver herself, so she would no doubt have a passing knowledge of other fences, if only by hearsay from sellers. Loop himself might have mentioned Berendsi at some time; he dealt with both."

Headlights and flashing blue lights topped out at the far end of the mesa. Bernice moved in beside Joe, rubbing her arm. "That's the cops for you. Never around when you need 'em."

Kendall's cruiser with the crumpled fender roared up and swung around and then disappeared, swallowed in its own dust cloud. Headlights bobbed and rocked to a halt in the haze behind it.

Tom studied the fallen doctor. "I met her at the post office at Second Mesa. She was asking about Rassah Someone. Why did she come here today?"

"I'd say it was to reach Hobasie before we did, or at least when we did. Personal contact would be the best way to reassure him that he wouldn't be sacrificed. She was surely afraid we'd find him and he'd spill."

Berendsi sneezed as Kendall's dust cloud floated over him. "What'd ya mean, 'If I touch silver I'm a dead man,' if it wasn't a trick?"

"Her main interest wasn't making a fortune in stolen silver, John. It was protecting the museum. She reached the top of its pile. In an important sense she *is* the museum. She couldn't let all that go down the tubes. You had just killed Carl Hobasie, and her reputation's spotless. As soon as you retrieved some silver—or tore apart enough hives to make the scene look good—she'd cut us all down. The only witnesses gone, she could construct a story that you killed us, and you would have killed her except that somehow she got the drop on you. She knew Kendall here was right behind. She gets off scot-free and you, the so-called murderer, lie dead."

They were getting quite an audience behind the dissipating dust cloud—Kendall, the tribal cop, other veiled heads. Tom was nodding as if he understood. "So far, so good. And ye say she killed Mouse and Loop?"

"Mouse said neither of them saw their attacker. I think Loop was guessing, based on his fight with Berendsi, and he guessed wrong. Unless, John, you really did pull the trigger."

"That Indian tonight was manslaughter. He got in my way. Got too uppity. But murder one? No way."

"I believe you. You're not dumb enough to commit first-degree murder—and a cop, to boot—to protect some theoretical windfall you haven't seen yet and might never see at all. Schumacher, though, saw her whole scheme fall through if Loop tipped the police. She had to act quickly."

Tom shook his head. "Nay, Jose. She was out at Bapchule. She couldn't have known Loop intended to squeal."

"I thought so too. But think: we reached her in less than three hours and we didn't know where we were going. We followed them back out in less than two. I suspect she left before dawn, for she and Sommers frequently went separate ways. She went into town to check the progress of her contrived burglary or perhaps complete arrangements. By chance she learned Loop was about to blow the lid because of Berendsi's big mouth. Did she use your loose tongue to extract the gun from you, John?"

"I ain't talking without a lawyer."

"A hole in your cognitations, me lad. How'd she know exactly where to set her trap? How'd she pick that upstairs window?"

"That stymied me, Tommy, until I learned this morning that Loop returned to Berendsi the morning he was shot."

"You can't prove that!" Berendsi exploded. "Lu Ella was asleep!"

"She was, and if Schumacher left her desert camp by 5 or so, she'd be in your apartment by 7. I'll bet she was there talking to you when Loop showed up. She heard him vow to take his tip to the cops, realized the danger he posed, and stalked him. She watched him make a phone call, then followed him two blocks. He stood around waiting; she picked her spot. Not an ideal spot, but adequate. She couldn't put Loop down and leave an armed police officer as witness and pursuer. Besides, she didn't know how much he had spilled on the phone. She silenced them both."

Tom wagged his head. "And hied herself back to her desert camp to set her alibi in cement."

Kendall started forward but Schumacher didn't look quite ready yet to relate to the rest of the world.

Joe stepped back. "Y'know, Tommy, Pete should be here. Not just the silver, which is his bailiwick. Mouse's killer. For his own sake, Pete needs to be in on this mop-up."

"Aye, you're right. He needs this more than we

do. Wish he were here."

"I am."

Joe's head snapped around and the sudden pain nearly blinded him. The dust was starting to settle; he could now see that headlights behind Kendall's cruiser were from a department black and white.

Pete Marks skirted the crumpled fender and brushed past Kendall. He stared at Schumacher a long, long moment. "When Mel Carter told me you two were both headed this way, I had to come. I was afraid you'd beat me to another one. Saw these cars running code three along the main road and figured you two would be in the mess somehow, so I followed." Pete tried to look at Joe, but his eyes averted. "What you two said about me just now—in the middle of all this you thought about what was good for me—I, uh . . ." Abruptly he walked away.

Tom grinned at Joe, widely and joyously.

In the thickening dusk Pete was saying, "What do you have here?"

Bernice bubbled. "It was all here in the beehives! Look! Bees go to sleep at night when it gets dark, but you have to be careful anyway. I just got stung." She lifted high a heavy squash-blossom necklace with a magnificent, turquoise-studded five-inch naja. For want of a better place to put it, she draped it around her neck and reached for something else.

Tom stepped in closer. "Your girlfriend there seems to be taking a healthy interest in life, despite herself. Nice to see."

"My girlfriend!"

"Meself be not blind to the ways of the world, Jose. When I rescued ye this afternoon, 'twas not merely the merciless desert I rescued ye from."

"You're a perceptive observer, Tommy." Joe looked at him, frowned, and looked again. He reached out and tipped Tom's face northwest, toward the brightest of the darkening sky. "Hey. How come you shaved off your moustache?"